Praise for *I Too Had a Love Story*

'In his book, Singh has beautifully portrayed various emotions of life and love, its trials and tribulations, victory and defeat'
—*The Indian Express*

'The past tense in the title is intriguing, as is the dedication: "To the loving memory of the girl whom I loved, yet could not marry." Ravinder's narrative is compelling, his emotions reflect a felt experience, and the denouement is touching. His tribute to the girl he loved will touch many a heart'
—*The Tribune*

'Ravinder's debut novel promises to strike a chord with the readers. While this poignant tale might not make you smile at the end, it will strengthen your belief in the fact that love stories are eternal'
—*The Times of India*

'The story is poignant and also real. Full credit goes to the writer, Ravinder Singh, who keeps the story focused. Everything is real in the book. The people, places and especially how they interact with one another. The book narrates a very important chapter in Ravin's life, but not without the message that the show must go on'
—*Metro News*

'They say, don't cry because it's over but instead smile because it happened. This inherent hope and optimism is what this book embodies. As we accompany Ravin on his journey to find happiness, we go through a range of emotions. From initial excitement to elation, from contentment to anticipation, despair to devastation and finally a sense of resurrection, we see it all through Ravin's eyes. *I Too Had a Love Story* is a simple story of love, about trysts of destiny that make up life as we know it. I commend Ravin on having the courage to share something so personal with the world.'
—Anupam Mittal, CMD and founder, Shaadi.com

'Simple, honest and touching'
—N.R. Narayana Murthy

T0314652

Ravinder Singh is the bestselling author of *I Too Had a Love Story*, *Can Love Happen Twice?*, *Like It Happened Yesterday*, *Your Dreams Are Mine Now* and *This Love That Feels Right*. He has an MBA from the renowned Indian School of Business and is based in New Delhi. Ravinder's eight-year-long IT career started with Infosys and came to a happy ending at Microsoft where he worked as a senior programme manager. One fine day he had an epiphany that writing books is more interesting than writing project plans. He called it a day at work and took to full-time writing. He has also started a publishing venture called Black Ink (www.BlackInkBooks.in) where he publishes debut authors. Ravinder loves playing snooker in his free time. He is also crazy about Punjabi music. You can reach out to him on his Twitter handle @_RavinderSingh_.

I too had a Love Story

RAVINDER SINGH

BLACK SWAN

TRANSWORLD PUBLISHERS
61–63 Uxbridge Road, London W5 5SA
www.penguin.co.uk

Transworld is part of the Penguin Random House group of companies
whose addresses can be found at global.penguinrandomhouse.com

 Penguin
Random House
UK

First published in India by Srishti Publishers and Distributors 2009
Published in Penguin Metro Reads by Penguin Books India 2012,
part of the Penguin Random House group of companies

First published in Great Britain in 2017 by Black Swan
an imprint of Transworld Publishers

A CIP catalogue record for this book
is available from the British Library.

ISBN
9781784163341

Typeset in Bembo by Eleven Arts, Delhi, India.
Printed and bound by Clays Ltd, Elcograf S.p.A.

Penguin Random House is committed to a sustainable
future for our business, our readers and our planet. This book is made from
Forest Stewardship Council® certified paper.

MIX
Paper | Supporting
responsible forestry
FSC® C018179

3 5 7 9 10 8 6 4

Not everyone in this world has the fate to cherish the fullest form of love. Some are born, just to experience the abbreviation of it.

Dedicated to

The loving memory of the girl whom I loved, yet could not marry.

Tere jaane ka asar kuch aisa hua mujh par,

tujhe dhoondate dhoondate, maine khud ko paa liya . . .

– Anonymous

. . . Otherwise, I wouldn't have come across an author in me.

Days pass by somehow
But nights now are a wagon of pain
Injuries may heal with time
But marks will always remain
Restless on my comfortable bed
I toss and turn and try to sleep
But thoughts are bulking my head
And have formed a huge heap
The past is flashing its scorching light beams
Tearing me apart, breaking me at the seams
The darkness of my life is more visible in the dark
And now I am trying to give it a voice, trying to speak my heart

Contents

Reunion

I remember the date well: 4 March 2006. I was in Kolkata and about to reach Happy's home. I had been very excited all morning as I was going to see our gang of four after three years. After our engineering, this was the first time when all of us—Manpreet, Amardeep, Happy and I—were going to be together. During our first year in the hostel, Happy and I were in different rooms on the fourth floor of the Block-A building. Being on the same floor, we were acquaintances but I never wanted to interact with him. I didn't think him to be 'a good guy' because of his fondness for fights and the red on his mark sheet. But, unfortunately, I was late in getting back to the hostel at the beginning of the second year and almost all the rooms were already allotted by then. I was not left with any choice other than becoming Happy's roommate. And because life is weird, things changed dramatically and, soon, we became the best of buddies. The day our reunion was scheduled, he had been working with TCS for two years and was enjoying his onsite project in London. Happy was blessed with a height of 6'1", a good physique and stunning looks.

And Happy was always happy. Manpreet, or MP as we called him, is short-statured, fair and healthy.

The reason I use the word 'healthy' is because he will kill

me if I use the proper word—'fat'—for him. He was the first among us to get a computer in the hostel and his machine was home to countless computer games. In fact, this was the very reason Happy and I wanted to be friends with him. MP was quite studious. He had even cracked the Maths Olympiad in his school days, and was always boasting about it. His native place was Modinagar but, at the time of this reunion, he was working with Ocwen in Bangalore.

Amardeep has been baptized 'Raamji' by MP. I don't know when he got this weird nickname or why, but it was probably because of his simple, sober nature. Unlike the rest of us at the hostel, he was not at all a night person and his room's light would go off precisely at 11 p.m. At times, MP, Happy and I used to stand outside his room a few seconds before 11 and begin to count down, '10, 9, 8, 7, 6, 5, 4, 3, 2, 1 . . . and Raamji has gone down.' The only mysterious thing about Amardeep was that he used to go somewhere on his bicycle, every Sunday. He never told us where he went. Whenever we tried to follow him, somehow he would know and would digress from his path to shake us off. Even today, none of us knows anything about it. The best thing about the guy, though, is his simplicity. And, very importantly, he was the topper in the final semester of our Engineering batch. He made our group shine. He belonged to Bareilly and was working with Evalueserve when he, along with MP, flew to Kolkata for the reunion.

After college, all of us were pretty much involved in our stereotypical lives. One day, we found out that Happy was coming back from London for two weeks. Everybody was game for a reunion. 'Happy's place in Kolkata, 4 March 2006,' we decided.

Finally, on the scheduled date, I was climbing the stairs to Happy's apartment two steps at a time. It was about 12.30 in the afternoon when I knocked on his door. His mom opened it and welcomed me in.

As I had often been there, she knew me well. For me, Happy's house never meant too many formalities. I was having some water when she told me that Happy was not at home and his cell was switched off.

'Wow! And he asked me not to be late,' I murmured to myself.

A little later, there was another knock on the door. I got up from my chair to open it, as Happy's mom was in the kitchen. I pulled it open to shouts of, 'Oh . . . Burrraaaaahhhh . . . Dude . . . Yeah . . . Huhaaaaaaaaa . . . Ohaaaaaaaaaaa!'

No, it wasn't Happy. MP and Amardeep had arrived.

Seeing your college friends after three years is so crazy and exciting that you don't even realize you are at someone else's place where you should show some manners and be polite. Then again, the very purpose of this reunion was to recall our college days and this was the perfect start. While we made ourselves comfortable on the sofas in the drawing-room, MP asked about Happy's whereabouts.

'He's not on time in his own home,' I said looking at MP and we laughed again.

For the next half hour or so, the three of us talked, laughed and made fun of each other while eating lunch made by Happy's mother. Yes, we started our meal without Happy. This might not sound decent, but we had genuine reason—nobody could predict his arrival, so there was no point in waiting.

A little later, there was another knock. Happy's mom opened the door.

'*Happy veeeeeeer!*' MP shouted, getting up from the dining chair.

Amardeep and I stared at each other. It seemed as if MP was going to shed tears as he hugged Happy. We remembered how these guys used to cry during their long boozing sessions, when their brains switched off and their hearts started speaking.

Amardeep and I used to enjoy our Coke, while seeing them getting senti.

We all stood up to hug him and as soon as that was done, we continued our lunch. Happy also joined us. The food that day was very tasty. Or maybe it was just because we were having lunch together after so long and that made it special.

After lunch, we moved to another flat, a few floors above, in the same building. This was the second flat which Happy's family owned, and was meant for relatives and friends like us. We were laughing at one of MP's jokes while moving in, and were probably still laughing as we fell on the giant couch in the drawing room—upside down—legs on the couch and our torsos on the floor, arms spread across and facing the ceiling; we made ourselves comfortable.

Nobody said anything for a few moments. And then it started again with Happy's big laugh. I guess he remembered some incident involving Raamji.

That evening, the four of us in that flat were having an amazing time. Talking about our past and present. About those not-so-goodlooking girls in college. About the porn we used to watch on our computer. About our experiences abroad and many other things.

'So which one did you like more, Europe or the States?' Happy asked me, getting up.

'Europe,' I replied, still lying down and looking at the ceiling.

'Why?' Amardeep asked. He always needed to find out the reason behind everything (though he never gave any reason for not telling us where he went every Sunday, during our hostel days).

'Europe has a history. The languages change when you leave one country and move to another. The food, the art and architecture, fabulous public transport, the scenic beauty, everything is just wonderful in Europe,' I tried to explain.

'You did not see all this in the US?'

'Some things, like public transport, are not that good in comparison to Europe. You and your car are the only options in most of the states, New York being an exception. You won't hear as many languages as you get to hear in Europe. I mean the US is damn advanced but still, I would prefer Europe to the States.'

Amardeep nodded and this meant his questions had ended.

'This is the best thing about IT jobs, Amardeep. We get to visit different places which we never dreamt of during our college days,' MP said to Amardeep. After college MP, Happy and I joined IT firms, while Amardeep joined the KPO industry. He had never liked the hardcore software business.

We were glad to be together again, finally, after the farewell night in college and we kept talking for hours that afternoon. We were planning an outing for the evening when we realized how tired we were and how badly we needed a little rest . . . I don't remember which one of us fell asleep first, that afternoon.

'Wake up, you asses. It's already 6.30.'

Someone was struggling to get us out from our utopia of dreams. In the hostel, Amardeep was the first among us to wake up and, of course, the only one to wake up others. So we knew that it was our early-morning Amardeep.

Still, how can somebody thumping your door to get you out of bed be pleasant? We human beings have such a weird nature—while asleep, we hate the person who is trying to wake us up, but once we are awake, we tend to love that same person because he did the right thing. As usual, Amardeep was successful in his endeavor. It was 7 in the evening.

This was the first time Amardeep and MP had come to the city, so we decided to explore the streets of Kolkata. Fortunately our host possessed two bikes—his own Pulsar and his younger brother's Splendor. We got ready and pulled out the bikes from the garage. MP and I got on the Splendor, Happy and Amardeep on the Pulsar.

We crossed the river Hooghly, over the Vidya Sagar Setu, shouting and talking to each other. Speed-breakers couldn't break our speed that evening. And where were we? On cloud number nine. Being with your best buddies after such a long time is, at once, sentimental and thrilling.

We went to the Victoria Memorial and few other places. At times, we got down to have some fruit-juice. At times, we halted to enjoy Kolkata's famous snacks and sweets. At times, we got down because one of us wanted to pee—which initiated a chain-reaction among the rest of us.

We were at some place, enjoying ice-tea in an earthen cup, when MP asked, 'When do we need to get back home?' It was already 10.30.

'No worries. I have the keys for the flat upstairs. We can go any time we want. Hopefully, we will not move in before 1,' Happy said, finishing his ice-tea down to the last drop.

'And where are we going to be till then?' Amardeep was concerned.

Amardeep and his 11 p.m. sleeping time, I remembered, but didn't bring it to the others' notice.

Happy looked at me and asked with a smile, 'Shall we go to the same place?'

'Oh! That one . . . ?' Before MP's dirty brain-cells could start thinking something filthy, I tried to clear the picture. 'Gentlemen! We are going to a very cool place now, and I bet both of you will find it . . .'

I was trying to finish when MP became impatient and cut me off, 'Oh yes. I heard that Chandramukhi was from West Bengal. So, are we guys planning to . . . ?' His wicked smile and naughty eyes completed the question.

'You're nuts,' Happy said, laughing.

'Don't think too much, MP. Just follow us,' I added.

Without revealing any more, we were back on our bikes, driving to our destination.

It wasn't yet midnight when we reached the place. The air here was a little colder. At first glance it looked as if we were in the slums. There was a run-down garage which was shuttered. Some trucks were parked outside. Their drivers were probably sleeping. We parked our bikes beside one of the trucks and walked through a small street to the right of the garage. The place was badly lit and utterly silent. Our voices and footsteps rang out loudly. The sounds of insects added to the eeriness of the place. MP heard a pack of dogs barking somewhere nearby. I don't know if he really heard them, though. Maybe it was just his poor heart, beating loudly.

'Shhh! They will wake up,' said Happy with a finger on his lips.

'Who?' Amardeep whispered.

'There are people sleeping on the ground ahead. Watch your step,' Happy said.

'People! Sleeping on the road?' Amardeep slowed down. They were local fishermen. Some were sleeping and some were hung-over from home-made liquor.

Suddenly, the street ended in a wooden channel. This was a staircase-like structure going down, and we could hear a dull sound, like that of water beating against the shore. We stepped on this channel leaving behind the insect-sounds.

In a few seconds, we were at our destination.

It was the river Hooghly, and we were standing at its bay. Amardeep's and MP's fear turned into delight.

'This is the Launch Ghat and, right now, we are in Howrah. This is the point from where the ferry takes you to the other side: Kolkata city,' Happy announced, pointing across the river.

In our excitement, we jumped onto the wooden harbor-like structure, from the channel. Surrounding this harbor on three sides was the river in its perfect velocity. It was a beautiful night, with the moon overhead and the stars shining bright. And beneath this sky, the four of us!

We sat down beside one of the giant anchors in a corner of the harbor. The river raced against the cool breeze to meet the Bay of Bengal. In the silence, the sound of water hitting the harbor was crystal clear. On the other side of the river was Kolkata. The tall buildings and the chain of tiny, yellow lights reminded me of the New York skyline. But this was much better, just because I was with my friends now.

With our arms wide open, we breathed deep and long, inhaling the fresh, chill air, still intoxicated by the beauty of this place. That was when Happy spoke up.

'So?' he asked, looking at Amardeep.

'What?' Amardeep asked in return, not understanding Happy's 'So.'

'So, how is this place, dammit?'

'Oh! This place? I cannot think of a better place than this. This is heaven.'

And then, again, a cool breeze blew, embracing us. We lay down on the harbor.

That was when the discussion started. A serious discussion; a discussion that changed my life. It started with another 'So'.

'So?' Amardeep asked this time, looking at Happy.

'What?' Happy asked, raising his chin.

'What's the next important thing?' Amardeep asked.

'You mean dinner?' MP jumped in.

'No, I mean the next important thing in life. Schooling—done. Engineering—done. Getting a good job—done. Going abroad—done. Bank balance—in progress. What's the next milestone?'

'Ah! I know what you're talking about,' Happy nodded. 'Ask him,' he said, pointing his already raised chin towards me.

Everyone looked at me.

'I don't know what's going on in your life and family, but my mom and dad are going crazy. They're after me like you wouldn't believe. Don't I make a good bachelor?' I said.

'The story is the same everywhere. We poor bachelors,' MP said trying to be funny.

'I am serious, MP,' Amardeep said.

'So, have you or your family fixed something?' I asked him.

'No. My story is just like yours. But the fact is that, one day, we'll have to settle down with a life-partner. How long can we ignore our parents' questions? They too have expectations, wishes and dreams for us.'

'I know what you mean Amardeep. But are you really ready to spend your whole life with someone? I mean, in our four years at the hostel, there were so many times when we had to adjust with each other . . . . This one will be for a lifetime,' Happy said.

'But, sooner or later, we have to do this, right?' Amardeep asked.

'What if we just carry on the way we are?' MP said.

'Then imagine yourself at the age of sixty, living alone. Life isn't that easy, my friend. It's a journey. And the best way to complete it is with a life-partner,' Amardeep said.

That night, on the bank of the river, the four of us discussed this issue seriously, for the first time. Maybe it was the first time we felt we were mature enough to talk about it. So many questions, ifs and buts were raised and answered between us. So many views were brought in and debated. None of us was against marriage but we wanted to evaluate its benefits. Amardeep and I were quite convinced about the marriage thing. And this discussion made Happy and MP think about the matter quite seriously, even it didn't convince them. (Which reminds me of a slogan I read on a T-shirt: *If you can't convince her, just confuse her!*)

'But then, other things come into the picture. Love marriage or arranged marriage? Parents' choice or ours?' Happy said.

'Now, that's a personal choice. But given that we are independent, I don't think our parents will object to our decision,' Amardeep said.

Happy kept mum hearing this.

'But Amardeep, look at our lives. All of us are North Indians, working in far-away states. The chance of finding a soul-mate, in this case, is quite slim. Moreover, the kinds of jobs we have don't give us the time to interact with different people. And above all, none of us would like to marry a girl chosen by our parents, if I am not wrong,' MP said.

'I don't know if your last statement is valid or not, but the rest is in your hands,' Amardeep replied.

'But MP has a point. In my case, I would like to marry a girl of my choice, but for the last one year I was abroad and I don't know if, in the next couple of years, I will be in India. Given this fact, it is quite hard for me to work on my marriage plan. And for a person like me it's impossible to settle down with any girl who is not Indian. Forget Indian, she has to be a Punjabi first of all,' I said.

'How did you apply for your job at Infosys?' Amardeep asked, digressing from the topic.

I answered, 'Through some job website.'

'And Happy, how did you transfer money from London to your parents?'

'Through my Internet banking account. It's quite fast,' he answered.

'See? The world is becoming Internet-savvy. And, given the fact that we all are IT graduates who are on the net almost everyday, why can't we use this for the marriage thing too?'

'Are you talking about matrimonial websites like Shaadi. com?' Happy asked.

'Yes.'

'Are they really useful? I don't think so,' MP put forward his view.

'To know if a dish is sweet or salty, you have to taste it first. That's the only way to know things for sure,' Amardeep answered.

'Or better yet, ask a person who has already tasted it. Why take a chance?' Happy said, trying to make us laugh.

'So Raamji, are you on any such website?' I asked.

'Not yet. But I'm thinking of it . . .'

When we did not say anything, he explained, 'The best thing about this service is that you can go through so many profiles without leaving your desk. The filters are good enough to provide you suitable matches. And you can interact with the persons who interest you . . . Everything is so systematic. Above all, you don't need to worry about your physical location . . .'

Amardeep made some valid points, which is probably why we didn't have much to debate about.

'Hmm . . . Well, I don't know if this thing is going to work, but it *is* worth giving a try. Who knows . . . ?' Even MP was convinced.

It was 1.30 a.m. Our empty stomachs reminded our brains of their existence.

Amardeep said, 'It's quite late and I'm damn hungry. Let's get home.' And he stood up stretching his back.

'So who's the first one?' MP asked while we all were dusting our clothes.

'The first one to marry? Or first one to make his profile on the website?' Happy asked, laughing.

'Both.'

'I think this guy,' Happy pointed his finger at me, I don't know why.

It was probably 4 a.m. by the time we had dinner and slept. And, after a long time, we enjoyed the kind of sleep we used to enjoy in our hostel. That day became one of the most memorable days in our lives.

We spent the next day visiting some of the best hangouts in Kolkata. And we went again to the Launch Ghat in the evening to ride the ferry to the other side of the city. And, believe you me, being on the ferry was no less amazing than boarding the Titanic in 1912. Being with your best friends is simply wonderful. We ate, drank, talked and enjoyed to the fullest at a pub called *Some Place Else*.

That was the last night of the reunion trip.

All three of them came to drop me at Howrah Station and, once again, the four of us hugged, just like we had at Hyderabad Station, on the last day of college.

'Who's going to cry first?' MP asked. But all of us laughed at that stupid and senti question.

The train called me with its final whistle. I got into the carriage and stood at the door, waving to them all as the train left the platform. I reached Bhubaneswar the next morning. That same morning, Amardeep and MP boarded flights back to their respective places. Soon afterwards, Happy also flew back to London.

Khushi

Three weeks later. I was in my office, just like on any other weekday. I was checking out the photos that MP had shot of us all, during the reunion trip. He emailed them to us and while I was looking at them, in my Yahoo! inbox, I noticed an ad flashing in the top-left corner.

It was an ad for a matrimonial site—Shaadi.com—with a beautiful girl, smiling and looking for her perfect match.

Recalling our reunion discussion, I clicked the hyperlink on this ad, which took me to the website. With the default filters enabled, I clicked the search button and, in no time, I was on the result page with many feminine pics. Wow! Some among them were damn pretty, and I wanted to check them all out. But before I could visit the sixth one, I was prompted to register at the website, without which I couldn't browse through more profiles. The trailer was over and to watch the whole movie you had to register yourself.

'I didn't have much work that day, so I thought I'd register myself and create my profile on the site.' This is what I kept saying to Happy, Amardeep and MP. Whereas, it was actually the other way round. Those pretty faces on the results page forced me to make time in my hectic schedule—which involved project delivery to a client, the very next day.

Someone rightly said, 'Three things—wealth, women and . . .' (I always forget the third one) '. . . can make anything happen in this world.'

So, finally, my profile was on the website. I uploaded a nice photograph and unchecked any checkbox which asked to hide my whereabouts from girls who might be searching for me. I did not forget to mention my professional trips to the US and Europe either. After an hour or so, I was all set to check out those pretty faces again. I set my filters to check out all the Punjabi girls on the website and hit the 'search' button.

The results page displayed some three-digit number—the total number of profiles that matched my search criteria. This was exciting! But I could only check out some fifty of them before my eyes grew tired. Still, among those fifty or so, there were a few whom I wanted to contact. But before I could do so, there came a heartbreaking moment. To talk to those pretty faces I had to make a payment to the site. There is no such thing as a free lunch. Damn!

The only cost-free part was a way to express my interest in them by clicking a button on their respective pages. This would send a message from me to their inbox. But even if they gave me an affirmation to interact, I still wouldn't get their email ids unless I made the payment. I checked the amount they were asking for. '3000 bucks for the yearly plan! No way,' I said to myself. Then I thought, 'I will only pay up if I happen to get good, affirmative responses from those beauties.' Till then, whenever I felt like it, I could ping any girl on the website to show my interest in her profile.

This was the beginning of my experience with Shaadi.com—at the cost of my project delivery, which I almost screwed up.

Apart from Happy, Amardeep and MP, nobody else knew about my profile on the site, not even my parents. Because telling them that I was thinking of getting married meant stirring a hornet's nest. The moment they found out, they would bring inputs from their acquaintances all over the planet—and, Jesus! How I hated that!

For the next few days, I got responses to my requests. Every time I opened my inbox there was this strange excitement. But, most of the time, it didn't last long. The best ones had declined me. In fact, most of them had ignored me. Only a handful accepted my request but, unfortunately, they didn't appear that good. 'Ah! This website is good for nothing,' I told myself. As if I was James Bond and all girls in the world would throw themselves at me, the moment I approached them.

And this is how Shaadi.com went from high-priority to the lowest-priority. Time passed by and I visited the site once in two or three weeks, clicking buttons on profiles that interested me, but without much expectation. Some more girls declined me; some girls, I declined. A few wanted to interact, but their education was not impressive. Some called me up on my cell; to some I wrote a few SMSs. A couple of them wanted me to move abroad but I was not game; some others, I could not convince that India was a better place to live in.

During one of my short, official trips to the US, I also happened to buy the yearly plan for a girl who badly wanted to talk to me. Damn! Out of the three things (wealth, women and . . . the last one which I always forget) that could make anything happen in this world, the second was already making me do things. The irony being that the girl, whom I coughed up 3000 bucks for, never got in touch. I lost all interest in the website.

Then, one evening, I received an SMS on my cellphone.

Hi I m Khushi I
received ur msgs
on my other cell can
u pls call me now

That was 20–July–2006 18:58:19. My cellphone's inbox still shows the date and time.

When I got this SMS, I was in a conference call with a client in the US. I quickly recalled the name of the profile from which I had got an acceptance the week before, along with the contact mobile number and an email id. I wrote an SMS in reply:

M in mid of a conf call.
wll ring you in another
hlf n hr.

The very next minute, my cell flashed the arrival of a new message.

I too hv cmpltd my conf cal
few min bck. U cmplete urs and
I can wait till then.

After finishing my call, I dialed her number but only after I had quickly browsed through her profile.

'Hello!' said a beautiful voice from the other end.

'Hi! This is Ravin.'

'And I am Khushi,' she said in a pleasing and confident voice.

'Yup, I learnt that in your SMS. Sorry I kept you waiting but I was in the middle of an important conference call with a client.'

'No problem. Even I had some stuff to complete.'

Our conversation began formally but, in no time, it became quite relaxed and informal when we found out some amusing things.

'I learnt that you were born in the month of February 1982,' she said.

'Yes. 4th February. Anything specific?' I wondered if I was supposed to recall something from her profile. But the only thing I remembered, then, was that she looked beautiful in her picture.

'You might have noticed that my year and month of birth are the same.'

'Oh yes! 22nd February. I had seen that,' I said, quickly rushing to my computer and scrolling through her profile. 'And you were born in Faridabad . . .'

'No. I was born in Kolkata. My dad was in the defence services and, when I was born, he was posted in Kolkata and was staying there with family.'

'Really . . . ? You won't believe this!' I shouted, attracting my coworkers' attention.

'What?'

'You guess!' I said, heading towards the staircase area, where I could talk to her without disturbing the others.

'Don't tell me you were also born in . . .'

But before she could complete her sentence, I shouted again, 'Yes!'

'But, how come?'

'That's my mother's native place.'

And I don't know why we screamed and laughed at this fact. Thousands of people must have been born in the same year, the same month and the same place, given our country's track record. But the way we reacted!

'You know, there is something else we have in common—the classical music thing. I learnt that you hold a degree in playing the sitar,' I said.

'Yes. And you hold one in playing the *tabla*, right?'

'Indeed. I learnt to play it for four years. In fact, I was never interested, but my dad forced me to . . .'

'Well, you know what? That's the only reason why I felt like contacting you.'

'I'm not sure I understand,' I said slowly.

'The hobby section in your profile said that you play the *tabla*. And your interest in classical music was the only thing that differentiated you from the others and made me feel like talking to you,' she clarified.

So that was it! A *tabla* makes a girl want to talk to a guy! It was impossible to understand girls, but I felt like hugging my dad and thanking him for forcing me to learn the *tabla*.

'Even I got my degree after four years at Prayaag University. And we both are in the IT industry,' she pointed out more things we had in common.

'Oh yes! You work with CSC Noida, if I am not wrong?' I asked, knowing that I wasn't wrong. And how could I be, when her profile was in front of me?

'Yes. I work with CSC . . . Tell me something. My friends say that Infosys people are studious and good rank-holders. Is that true?'

'Are you expecting me to say 'no' to that?'

She laughed.

That was my first ever candid talk with a girl I hadn't seen yet. On that call, we touched base on various things: the latest movies we had seen, our best friends, her family, my family, our college days, music and other areas of interest.

'So is your family in Bhubaneswar too?'

'No, my native place is a very small town called Burla, near Sambalpur. Mom and dad live there. My brother and I are in Bhubaneswar, and we both work with Infosys. We stay in a rented flat with two other roommates, and visit our parents on alternate weekends. Burla is just a night's ride from Bhubaneswar.'

We talked for nearly an hour. I could feel my cellphone burning my ear, and the cell's battery was on its last legs. And even though I wanted to keep talking to her, I had to say, 'Listen! My battery is going to give up soon. But I hope we are going to stay in touch.'

'Your battery?' she said, laughing.

'I mean, my mobile's.' I started laughing too.

'Just kidding. But I believe we'll talk again.' Then she added, suddenly, 'But before you hang up, you have to say one good thing.'

One good thing? Now where on earth would I find one good thing to say? But I'd watched a movie the day before and, thanking god, I repeated a line from it. '*Bismil ka sandesh hai ki kal Lahore jaane wali gaadi hum Kakori pe lootenge, aur un paison se hathiyar kharidenge.*'

Then, I took a deep breath, and waited . . . And she burst into a big laugh.

I still think it was a good line. But I don't know what made her laugh. Anyhow, I too joined in her laughter, so that she would not think me stupid or lacking a sense of humor.

'OK! I'm hearing the final beeps from my cell. It was really nice talking to you, Khushi. But we won't be able to talk more, though I want to.'

'Same here. I liked talking to you very much. See you.'

'Yeah, bye.'

'Instead of bye, you should say 'see you'. It's nicer. It means we'll interact again . . .' she said, and touched my heart, somewhere. Her innocence and the candid way in which she talked to me had left its mark on my mind.

'See you,' I said, before I hung up.

That night, lying on my bed, I went over the conversation again and again. And I wondered: Could I have been more humorous, just to impress her further? Or was the call just perfect, the way it should have been? And was she thinking about the conversation too, at that very moment, sitting somewhere in her room.

I don't know why, but I felt like calling her up again and it was hard to curb that urge. But I had to control it, because I did not want to mess things up, right in the beginning, by becoming a guy who bothers her at 11.30 in the night. 'No,' I said to myself, loudly, switched off the light and jumped into bed.

Alone in my room, I was smiling, talking to nobody and there was this different sort of feeling within me. I slept, just so that the night would pass, and a new day would come when I could hear her beautiful voice once again.

The next day, I waited for her call. Though we'd not decided that she was supposed to call me, still I had this gut-feeling that she would. By 10, in the office I was getting restless. I wanted to hear her voice but, at the same time, I wanted *her* to call me up.

Happy had given me this success funda in the matter of girls: *Don't make them feel that you are going crazy after them; just give some time and they will come to you.*

At 11, I realized that Happy was a fool and I went ahead and SMSed her a 'good morning', even though it was a little late for that. But I didn't receive any reply to my SMS and began wondering who the real fool was . . .

And, that day, I was also uncertain. Should I listen to my heart or my brain? Both of them were pointing in opposite directions. My brain was telling my ego, 'What does she think of herself?' Whereas, my heart still wished to hear her voice.

Call it my weakness or my effort to curb my ego—a little later I did what my heart told me to do and I dialed her number.

'Hey! Hi, how are you?' Khushi picked up the phone.

'When wishing you a good morning, the sender also expects a similar response. I am fine.'

'I was going to reply on the way to the office.'

'You mean you're still at home?'

'Yeah. Actually, we work in the afternoon shift as we have to be in sync with our UK-based clients. Hey, my cab's outside,' she said rushing and saying 'bye' to her mom. I could hear the door being closed and her 'hi' to her friends in the cab. After she got in, we resumed our talk.

'So what's up?' I asked her.

'Ami di was here this morning,' she said. I remembered her mentioning a couple of names during our previous call, but I could hardly remember who was who among them.

'Ami di . . . ?' I murmured, trying to recall the name.

'I have three sisters and one brother. Misha di is the eldest and lives in Ludhiana. She has a very sweet kid, Daan, who is studying in nursery. Ami di is the second, and she too is married. She lives in Noida, an hour's drive from our place, and works with a BPO. Deepu, my brother, is two years younger than me and is working with an MNC in Assam. They deal with oil wells and stuff. And Neeru is the youngest, my sweet little sis,' she told me about her siblings again, with no complaints or questions as to how I forgot about them so soon.

She continued, 'And apart from this, mum and dad are with us. And in your family, it's your mom and dad, you and your younger brother, Tinku, who is also a software engineer with Infosys, and his office is in the same building as yours, except he is on the first floor and you on the second. Right?'

And that was a silent slap to my memory. She remembered everything about my family. All I could do was say, 'Hmm . . . 10 on 10,' and laugh. But I laughed alone.

'So, I was saying, Ami di was here this morning. After completing her night-shift she came to Faridabad. She visits us once in a week or two.'

This call was all about her family. I came to know about two more people—Davinder Jiju, Misha di's husband, and Pushkar, Ami di's husband. Pushkar and Ami di used to work in the same company and they happened to fall in love, which was not a good idea according to Khushi's dad. The hurdles they had to face were no different from any love story in Bollywood movies. Pushkar comes from a Hindu family whereas Ami di belongs to a Sikh family. Pushkar is cool with boozing and non-veg while these things are taboo in Khushi's family. But then, as we learn from those same movies, Love, in the end, wins all the battles. And, that is what happened here as well. All the youngsters in Khushi's family successfully convinced their dad to give his approval for the marriage.

In that call, Khushi also mentioned that she used to leave her office around 9.30 at night and reach her home by 11. Which meant that she would be awake for quite a while and I could call her late at night in case I felt the way I had the night before.

So that was how we started calling each other, writing messages, even wishing each other goodnight. But, in our initial calls, we never touched upon the purpose for which we had started interacting—marriage.

But she initiated this, one day, when I forwarded her an e-album of my pictures, with my friends, in Belgium.

'I noticed one pic with the description—enjoying red wine in a pub,' she said.

'Oh yes, that was one of the happening evenings in Belgium.'

'So you booze?'

'Hmm . . . yeah. But very rarely. Once in two or three months, or at times six. Only on some occasions when I am with friends and they insist I give them company,' I answered coolly.

'Well, I don't know how you are going to react on this, but I always wanted a life-partner who abstains from this.'

And I asked myself, 'So, is she saying that she is going to look for somebody else?' I wasn't sure. But the one thing I was sure about was that, finally, we were discussing marriage.

She continued, 'See, every person has some likes and dislikes. When we talk about marriage, it's about respecting each other's feelings; it's about trust, a few compromises and much more. And if you are going to be my life-partner, I sincerely urge you to choose a life without alcohol.'

She was the first among us to say: *if you are going to be my life-partner.* And in her voice those words sounded so different, so magical.

And, of course, it was the magic of those words which overrode my consciousness and made me say, 'It's a gentleman's promise. If you are going to be my life-partner, I will not booze unless you are comfortable about it. And I mean it.' I didn't stop there but continued, 'The reason I can do this is because alcohol is not something I am addicted to. At the same time, I don't think it's bad to booze once in hundred days, just to give company to your best friends. Even then, I have never crossed my limits and got drunk completely. Still, if this becomes a problem between me and my life-partner, I will gladly abstain.'

'And promises are meant to be kept . . .' she reiterated. And, probably, she smiled too.

'Absolutely!' The gentleman within me was still talking. 'But the day you get to know me completely—after six months, or ten, or maybe a year, or maybe more than that. Then, if you think that boozing is not at all a bad case with me, you will have to allow me to have a drink with my best friends. But, again, I will never force you to say that.'

This was another landmark in our saga and, henceforth, she felt much better talking to me. And I felt good, just because she felt good.

Was the second, out of the three things (wealth, women, and I still can't remember the third) that could make anything happen in this world, making me do this? I didn't know then, and I don't know now. The only thing bothering me was, what would I say to Happy and MP when we sat together with red wine, at our next reunion? 'Guys, please bear with me as I've stopped boozing because of a promise I made to a girl, whom I've only talked to on the phone for a week. Yes, only a week. Far lesser time than the years which we all have spent together.'

I didn't know, then, if that promise was good or bad for me. But what was definitely good was the trust and understanding we gained. And this was just beginning. It was a tough call . . . But then, something within me wanted her for a long, long time . . . Forever.

Another Step Closer

'What? You haven't talked to your parents yet? Shona! You promised me you'd do that by now.'

If you are wondering who this new character, Shona, is—it's me. And the person shouting those questions at me is my Khushi. Yes, she is mine now.

We are in love. For the first time . . . Sounds crazy?

So, did it happen when we were studying together in college?

Of course not. I am a thousand miles away from her.

Was it love at first sight?

Definitely not. We haven't even seen each other yet!

—The questions my friends would ask me, and the answers I gave them. (There were some dirty ones too, which I can ignore.) But everyone's last question was the same.

Are you crazy?

I don't knnoooowwww . . .

Indeed, being in love with a person you haven't even met is a crazy thing. And deciding to marry that person some day, even crazier. Never in my wildest dreams had I thought my love-life would be like this. To be honest, I had never even thought of any love-life.

But, now, I had changed a lot and was no longer the person I used to be till some time ago.

A lot of things had changed, in me and around me. I had started slipping out of conversations with my friends just to give her a call. I slept less and talked more. My phone bills led my monthly spending chart, leaving the house rent miles behind in the race. I started noticing couples: the way they sat together in gardens, hand in hand; the way a girl holds her boyfriend, on a motorbike. I started worrying about the 'how do I look' factor. My status on Orkut changed from 'single' to 'committed'. She became the password to my several Internet IDs. Sitting in my office alone, I used to smile, talking to nobody.

Love was in the air.

Ours was such a different story. A 21st century love story, whose foundation was modern-day gadgetry. Thanks to Graham Bell for inventing telephones that helped me talk to her, know her better and, finally, fall in love with her. Thanks to the Internet, the World Wide Web and sites like Shaadi.com that helped me find her. I discovered myself to be a true software engineer in this hi-tech-love phase. And whether this kind of love was good or bad, was no longer a point to ponder—we were already in it.

Coming back to the reason she was shouting at me.

It was because I had broken a promise. No, not the boozing one. Something else.

Her family knew about me since our first call, but the case wasn't the same at my end. My family did not know about her yet. In fact, they didn't even know that their son's profile was on some matrimonial site. Naturally, she was concerned about this situation. That too, after we had finally decided our destiny.

Her queries about this matter were growing everyday. Gradually, she started feeling uncomfortable because of this very reason. Therefore, a week earlier, I had promised her that I would talk to my family on the coming weekend. But unfortunately, I could not, because of the weekend exam at

IMS. (IMS. Another interesting similarity between us was this MBA preparation center. We both were preparing for MBA, and we had joined the same crash-course in the same institute in our respective cities!)

'I could not travel to Burla last weekend because I had to appear for a test at IMS,' I said, trying to calm her.

'But you promised me Shona . . . !' My shouting lady turned into an emotional one. She killed me with that name. She loved to call me different names and the best among them all was Shona. And I loved the way she used to say it. With such care and warmth.

'This weekend I will, for sure. I don't have any task more important than this one,' I told her.

And my Shonimoni was happy again. Shonimoni. The name I gave her. Punjabi for cute and sweet; the feminine counterpart to Shona.

The next weekend arrived and I was panicking. After all, I was going to talk to my parents about my marriage. This was definitely going to be a bolt from the blue, for them.

I was smart enough to take my younger brother, Tinku, into confidence the night before we left for Burla. He already knew something was going on between me and some girl. My late night calls had made that much clear. But he had never imagined that all this started at a matrimonial site. Being his elder brother, I did not give him any option except to be on my side when I talked to mom and dad.

Since the moment we arrived at our home in Burla, I was doing strange things, moving here and there, trying to bring the subject up, trying to find just the right moment. But I was not at all sure what the perfect moment was.

I was thinking too much. More than my brain could handle. Should I say it now? Or should I wait till the clock's minute hand has covered fifteen more minutes? But even after it had covered a hundred and fifty minutes, I was still waiting.

Every time I was about to spill it out, something would happen: the telephone rang, somebody knocked at the door and, if nothing else, the stupid pressure cooker's whistle dragged my mom back into the kitchen. The one moment when no such thing happened, I just could not open my mouth.

'She's going to cry this time, if I don't do this,' I told myself.

After lunch, I somehow gathered enough courage to initiate the dreaded conversation. Even though I thought it was quite bizarre to ask my parents how they met and married each other, I could not think of a better way to bring up the subject.

'Mumma, tell me one thing. How did you guys find each other and end up marrying?' I asked.

Mom and dad looked at each other, then at me and smiled. Parents are smart, and what we don't know is that they know what is going on in our minds. They had probably read, very easily, what the marquee on my forehead was displaying.

Still, they narrated their story, and the moment that was over, Mumma asked, 'So how is yours getting started?'

I wondered if I should hide my face in the cushions, or say, 'My story . . . ? I don't have any,' before my brain angrily told me, 'Come on, speak up, you fool!'

And, fortunately, gathering all my shy courage, I narrated my story so far. I even showed them her picture. I was expecting a lot of ifs and buts from my parents, but to my surprise nothing of that sort happened. Even Tinku had asked me more questions than my parents asked!

Mom was happy because, finally, her son was thinking about marriage. Dad was happy because the toughest part—searching for a girl of his son's choice—was over. He was relieved, though he tried to sound quite diplomatic. I was happy because, finally, I was able to get this thing out of my heart and place it in front of everybody. And Tinku, he was observing everybody's reactions. He doesn't get influenced easily, and that's something I both like and dislike in him.

A couple of questions from both mom and dad, which I answered with confidence, and that was it. I had never thought that this toughest of hurdles would be over so quickly.

But before we left for Bhubaneswar, on Sunday night, at the bus stop, dad said, 'We will analyse this, but it's good that you have become serious about your marriage.'

'No issues. I understand your point,' I said to him. Inside, though, I was thinking, 'Who cares Dad!'

Monday morning, I reached my other home in Bhubaneswar. Stretching out on my bed, I called Khushi up.

'Mission accomplished,' I said, waking her up. Those two words conveyed everything to her. And what did I get in response? A fusillade of kisses. The last ones were real passionate. That was the first time she kissed me on phone.

'Oh boy! So loud? No one is around, *haan*?' I asked.

She didn't answer my question but said, 'I feel like pulling you into my bed right now and kissing you madly.'

Wow! She was so happy, mad and comfortable, knowing that I had finally told my family about her.

Another milestone in our love story was crossed. Both our families now knew about our affair. And, as usual, I was happy because my Shonimoni was happy. But, as they say, 'Love is a blend of different emotions.' Soon an evening came when I made her cry. And then I cried because she was crying.

It was another weekend and I was in Burla, sitting in the verandah, busy with my Reading Comprehension—RC—section. I was annoyed, having scored rather badly in my self-exam. I was about to advance to the next passage when she called.

'Hey, hi . . .' I said in a depressed tone.

'What is my baby doing?' she asked. I loved it when she talked that way, when she called me 'baby' in her cutest voice. It sounded so caring. As if she had taken over all the responsibility of looking after me.

'RC is screwing up your baby and I'm in a very bad mood.'

'Then talk to me for a while and you'll be in a good mood again.'

'No dear. I want to start a new passage and score better this time. Only that will change my mood. Can we talk at night . . . please?'

'Hmm . . . Ok. See you later. But at least say one good thing before hanging up.'

There were so many things specific to Khushi, the little things that were important to her. Like this unique idea of listening to one good thing before we hung up. I liked it, most of the time, unless I was too tired to think up something new and good for her.

'Khushi! Please understand. My mind isn't working. I can't think of anything good at this moment. I'll tell you two good things at night. Ok?'

'Ok. You take care.'

'Bye.'

'Bye *nahin*, see you,' she corrected me again.

'Oh yes. See you,' and I hung up, still in a bad mood.

Hardly fifteen minutes had passed when I heard my cellphone ringing again. It was her.

'Now what?' My voice was a little loud.

'You know why I called you earlier?'

'Oho . . . ! Why?' I was annoyed.

'Because it's raining here. And I feel like holding your hands and dancing in the rain.'

'Khushi!' My voice grew louder.

'Ok *baba*, I'm sorry. See you later,' she said, innocently.

She was about to hang up when I felt bad about how I behaved and said, 'Hey wait. We can talk for a while. I needed a break from this damned RC thing.'

And she was happy again.

In a little while, the focus of our conversation changed from rain to our promises and priorities. The things we wanted to accept and the things we wanted to give up, for each other. No boozing until she was comfortable with it, preparing myself for a vegetarian environment (at least at home) and a few others things were on my plate. And talking to me and my family in Punjabi was the most important task I put on her plate. (Her family spoke Hindi and she was brought up in that atmosphere. Whereas, my ears badly wanted to hear the language which I was brought up around.) None of our expectations were forced upon each other, though. It was mutual understanding, an attempt to do the best we could for each other. After all, we were supposed to live together for the rest of our lives.

That evening, I asked her mischievously, 'Hey! Do you mind talking in Punjabi? I never heard you fulfilling my expectations. Or are you going to start after our marriage?'

'And if I say I won't do that even after our marriage, what will you do?' she teased me and laughed. I imagined her jumping off her bed and running to the window to catch a few raindrops.

'Then I'll take you back to your home in Faridabad and leave you there.'

All she said was, 'Shona . . . ?' I could hear the rain falling on the ground outside her window. I realized what I landed up saying. My attempt at humor had badly failed. I did not know how to react. Before I could say anything, she said, 'Shona, you carry on with the passage. See you later.' And she hung up very quietly—something she never did.

I felt very uncomfortable, recalling the way I had reacted to her teasing. I could neither call her up to tell her that I didn't mean what she thought I meant, nor could I concentrate on my RC passages. All my answers for the next passage were incorrect.

Later that evening, around 7 p.m., I rode my bike to the nearest ATM to get some cash for my ticket back to Bhubaneswar. It started drizzling—the first rain of the season. Now I could imagine how she felt when she had called me earlier. I got out of the queue in front of the ATM and dialed her number.

'Hello?' she said. Her voice was shaking.

'Khushi,' I said.

'Yes, Shona,' she promptly responded. Then I heard a choking noise which was enough for anyone to realize that she was crying.

I could not say anything for a moment, during which her tears rolled down further. 'Hey dear! Please . . . Please don't cry. I'm so sorry for having said those terrible words.'

She started sobbing loudly and I felt very ashamed for what I had done to the girl who wanted to hold my hands and dance with me in the rain. I felt as if I had committed the greatest sin—making the sweetest girl on earth, who was only meant for me, cry. How could I have done that? I hit the wall in front of me very hard. The people in the queue looked at me. I moved down the street to where there was no light.

'I am so sorry, Khushi. I am so sorry. Please don't cry because of my stupid mistake.'

Silence.

'Talk to me dear. Say something. Punish me but, for God's sake, talk to me,' and with that I too started crying.

After a while she managed to say, 'Shona, you haven't even taken me to your home yet and you're talking of sending me back.'

Her simple, innocent question left me speechless. She was crying, I was crying and the sky was crying with us. It started raining heavily.

'It took you just a second to say that. But I am a girl. I will be leaving my parents, my brother and sisters, people with whom I have lived my life so far, my home, which holds so many memories, just to become yours. And you said that you will leave me.'

'I'm stupid, I'm terrible. I really am,' I shouted, hitting a pole on the side of the street, crying loudly in that rain, not caring if anybody saw me. The clouds thundered. The rain came down hard and noisy. And I kept hitting the pole and crying. There must have been something wrong with me, for I had never cried that way.

And it's probably the nature of the feminine heart to stop others from crying. So she did what I should have done for her. She wiped my tears first.

'Shona! Shona . . . Please! I can hear you crying. Please don't do that. Please . . . See, I'm talking to you. And no matter what, I am yours, just yours and even now I am with you. And if you want to see me happy, please don't cry, my dear.' The broken heart was comforting the heart that had broken it. She even made me laugh a little, later.

Then I said, 'I feel sorry and I'm ashamed of myself for hurting you.'

'Shona, do you know that, just like you, I too want to be with my family for ever. But because of the way our society and culture is, I have to leave them all. And I will do that, because I am in love with you and the person I need the most for the rest of my life, to take care of me, is you.'

'I know that dear. I know that very well. I don't know how I landed up saying that. I never felt it from my heart. You have all the right to punish me.'

'Punishment?' she asked in a cute voice.

'Yeah. It can be anything,' I said.

'Where are you?' she asked, and I felt her voice getting better.

'I came to get some cash from the ATM. It's two blocks away.'

'Are there people at the ATM?'

'Yeah, there is a long queue.'

'Go back to the ATM queue.'

'Why?'

'Just go there. It's part of your punishment.'

'All right,' I said and went back. 'Yes. I am there.'

'Ok. Now give me five kisses.'

'What!?'

'Shona!' she said sternly, reminding me that I could not back out.

I had made her cry, and now I had to do what she wanted. I steeled myself and, ignoring the people around me, went ahead and gave her five loud kisses over the phone. I was the second last person in the queue and I kept my head bent to avoid contact with the surprised eyes which were staring at me.

It was embarrassing, to say the least, but she just laughed. And despite my embarrassment, I was happy to make her laugh again.

At the same time, I understood a girl's situation, the sacrifices she makes for the man of her dreams. She leaves behind everything she possessed so far in life, to embrace him and his family. I asked myself how I would have felt if I was to leave my family for her. Could I even think of leaving my family? How do girls do it? And, more importantly, why do only they have to do it? I didn't have any answers. In due course of time, Khushi taught me several such lessons. Gradually, she was changing me and my mindset.

That evening, I did not withdraw any cash because the next moment, I noticed one of my neighbors standing in the queue, right ahead of me. His face made it clear that he had caught me kissing my phone.

~

It is midnight, the last Saturday of August. I have come back home after watching a movie. Khushi and I had a quarrel in the afternoon and, because I couldn't stand not talking to her, I went to watch a movie, thinking it would make me feel better. It did not.

Unable to stand it any longer, I call her up in the middle of the night.

She picks up my call with a laugh, making me realize that I couldn't stand by my tough words—I said I would not be the first one to start talking again. Moments later, even I join in her laughter. We are no longer quarreling. Later, she says something that touches my heart.

'Shona! Let's make this a rule for our life after marriage. If we are together at home, then we will have dinner in the same plate, no matter what. Even if we had a terrible fight that day. We may not speak to each other, but sitting together . . . waiting for our turns to break the next bite of chapatti . . . the inadvertent touch of our hands as we eat . . . all this will calm our anger. Hai na?'

~

It was the beginning of October—almost three months since we knew each other. I had talked to her entire family by then, and she had talked to mine.

In fact, she had become a good friend of my mother. Mumma always wanted to have a daughter. Gradually, she started sharing her joys and sorrows with Khushi. She used to talk about my childhood, my nature, my likes and dislikes, the things that made me angry. She also talked about her life in this family, a family in which men outnumbered women by a ratio of 3:1 and where, unfortunately, the majority dominated.

There were things about my mother which I had never known earlier. But Khushi would tell me those things. Like any other son, I also love my mother, but the problem is that we never know when we become part of this male dominant society. Khushi used to explain to me the nature of a woman and her expectations. She used to tell me what I should do for her when I went back home, on weekends. She used to give me tips. At times, she also used to shout at me if I forgot them. I had one more reason to be happy then, for Khushi understood the importance of relationships, she knew the importance of family and how to care for it.

One more responsibility that I had given her was to neither call me up after 10 p.m., nor talk to me if at all I happened to call her up after that time. The reason was that the CAT exam was close and I wanted to devote three-four hours a day for preparation.

So, we took a vow, albeit reluctantly.

'Till the CAT is over, we will not talk to each other after 10 p.m.,' I said.

'. . . And this rule will only be followed on weekdays,' she added her clause, reasoning that on weekends we have surplus time to prepare and didn't need to make our lives tougher by not talking to each other.

'Ok *baba*. Now repeat after me,' I said.

'In the name of God, I, Ravin . . .' I paused for her to repeat after me.

'In the name of God my Shona and I, Khushi . . .' And I felt so good for the 'my Shona' in her statement. Inside, I felt like kissing her one more time for these small but wonderful things she often did for me. Outside, I went ahead with my vow.

'. . . take a vow that . . .' '. . . take a vow that . . .' '. . . we will not call each other on weekdays after 10 p.m., unless there is some kind of emergency . . .'

'. . . we will not call each other on weekdays after 10 p.m., unless there is some kind of emergency . . . and even if there is no emergency but, somehow, I am not able to sleep, I will only call you for five minutes,' she added another clause to the vow.

'What is this . . . ?' I asked, and laughed. Not being able to hold back my love for her, I kissed her. One after another, those kisses flew all the way to her place, bypassing so many mobile towers and satellites.

Khushi made me enjoy every moment of my life: the good, the bad, the challenging. She made them all simply wonderful.

The first week, it was quite tough to abide by our vow but, somehow, we managed. The truth was that, because of this vow, the urge to talk to each other, especially after 10 at night, increased even more—it is human tendency to desire what is prohibited. And during our morning calls, we realized that night was such a beautiful time to talk to each other.

'Talking at night used to be so romantic *na*?' she asked in her cute, innocent voice one morning.

'I miss them so much. This decision makes me feel like I've struck my foot with an axe, by mistake,' I said.

'No dear, it's not like you've struck your foot with an axe,' she started politely, then suddenly shouted, 'Rather your foot wanted to lick that axe and, willingly, you jumped on a sharpened one, that too barefoot! Now enjoy your wounds.' She was fuming.

But nothing could be done. Promises are meant to be kept, and we both knew we had to keep this one.

Soon, the weekend night came and we were desperate to talk to each other.

Night! Night is really a beautiful time to talk, for love-birds. Parents are asleep by then. Siblings understand why they should not disturb you. And you? Holding your cellphone, you are alone in your bedroom, lying on your cosy bed in your shorts and a comfortable T-shirt, with the lights dimmed. Which means, you are completely with the person you are talking to.

'Hi Shona,' she said.

There was something different in her 'hi' that night. Something passionate, something I'd rarely felt before.

'Hi honey,' I responded calmly, and we began talking. I remember how good we felt talking to each other at night after so long, though it had just been a week. A little later, she was telling me about her friend's engagement and, in a short while, she was talking about what our engagement would be like.

'The engagement will be at our premises, and I will be wearing a sari that evening. You know, why? Coz I look stunning in a sari,' she answered her question, before I could.

'Aha . . . *Chalo*, in that case, I want to see my Shonimoni in a sari that evening.'

'It will be one of the best evenings of my life. I will be standing beside my fiancée, amid so many people. I can touch you, hold your hand in front of everyone and nobody will say anything,' she said.

'I am dying for that evening to come. Then I will hold your hand and we will dance to the music, in front of everybody. I want my friends to be jealous because I possess you,' I said dreaming of that day soon to come.

'And, in everybody's presence, our eyes will be talking to each other.

Those unsaid words which will be heard very clearly by them. When you will look into my eyes, you will understand what I am feeling, that very moment, gazing at you.'

'And when the people will be busy helping themselves to the food, my eyes will ask you to come upstairs, to the terrace. And I will make my way to the staircase and head upwards.'

'And my eyes will tell you to go on ahead, and at the first opportunity, I will soon escape, saying I have to go to washroom,' she said, in that girlish, mischievous tone.

'I will be on the terrace, standing just behind the door where the staircase to the terrace ends.'

'You will hear my anklets and my bangles tinkling as I come up the stairs to the dark terrace,' she said, slowly.

'But you won't know that I am standing behind the door,' I whispered.

'And I will push the door and go straight ahead,' she too started whispering.

'The moment you go two steps ahead, I will grab you from behind.'

I don't know what was happening to us. Was it the fruit of spending those weeknights without talking to each other, or something else?

Outside, it had started raining, adding to the sensation of the moment. I could hear the rain spattering on the ground, and the cold breeze blew open the windows and came into my room that night.

'Shona!' she cried my name with pleasure.

'And grabbing you from behind, I will take you and lock you in my arms.' I closed my eyes. And maybe she did the same when she said, 'Shona!' again, very slowly, full of love, taking a deep breath.

'And with my hand I will bring your long hair in front of your left shoulder and I will bring my face very close to your neck on the right, with my other hand playing on your bare waist . . .'

I tried to keep my emotions in check because I did not want to scare my sweetheart too much, so early. She didn't say anything for a while, but our breaths were getting louder. My own heart was pounding inside me with pleasure.

'And then?' she finally asked. I understood her state of mind, the ripples, the troughs and crests in her heart. But, above all, she wanted to enjoy that moment with me.

And I answered her, 'And then you will feel my lips behind your right ear, on your neck.'

'Mmm,' she murmured, breathing heavily.

'I am feeling something so different at this moment. Are you?' I asked her very silently.

'Yes, something very different. What are you feeling?'

'With you in my arms, I am able to smell the cologne that you are wearing, your sweet feminine fragrance. I feel my lips kissing your shoulder and going down your back, licking the slightest sweat adhering to you . . .' By this time, even my voice had started shaking. I asked her, 'Tell me, what are you feeling?'

'I feel . . .' she was struggling to complete her sentence and I could still hear her breath loud and clear.

She hesitated. I waited.

'I . . . I feel,' she paused and then tried again, 'I feel as if you are hypnotizing me, casting a magic spell that I don't want to come out of.'

She was breathing faster now, shivering. Her passionate voice was stimulating me further.

'Now my other hand is moving on your waist. And then . . .' I paused.

'And then . . . ?' she insisted I go on.

'And then, all of a sudden, it has started raining,' I brought the rain from outside my window into our sweet dream.

'Mmm . . . And then . . . ?'

Very slowly, I whispered, 'And then, I have turned you towards me. We are wet from the rain. I am watching you in your wet sari which is sticking to your body. I am seeing the raindrops falling on your forehead, running down your nose and hanging on your lips for a while before running further down your body. Strands of your wet hair are glued to your cheek.'

'And then . . . ?' She started whispering again.

'You are looking down, somewhere on my shirt, too shy to look into my eyes. I am raising your chin, to help you look into and read my eyes which are staring at you.'

'A . . . n . . . d . . . t . . . h . . . e . . . n . . . ?' she was hardly able to speak any more and was losing her words.

'With our heads tilted slightly, my lips feel the raindrops sticking to your lips, swallowing them, further discovering the softness of your lips . . .' And that passionate kiss which I described to her lasted for quite a while. That was the first time, I felt, she allowed me to cross a few boundaries. Miles apart from each other, we felt each and every shiver of that moment.

We were lost in each other when, suddenly, she turned mischievous. 'Hey! People down there will be looking for us. I have to rush before my parents come upstairs, searching for me,' she shouted.

I wonder how she collected her energy and, more than that, how she remembered the fake people in the fake rain, on that fake engagement night (though it was to come true, in a few months).

'Aah! The people down there will be happy with their food,' I tried to convince her.

'Nah . . . please. Come on dear, now open your arms. We have to go and change our clothes before they see us,' she urged, laughing at the virtual reality we were in.

'Ok. But on one condition.'

'And what's that?'

'I want to see you while you change.'

'Oh . . . ho . . . ho . . . *tumhe ungli kya pakdaai, tum to pura haath pakdna chahte ho. Zyaada galat fehmiyaan mat paalo,*' she warned me with a little laugh.

'*Haath pakdna?* Not just the hand, I want to hold *all* of you!' I responded. I tried hard to convince her, but she didn't allow me, even though it was only make believe.

That night, we slept quite late. No, it wasn't night. I guess it was close to sunrise when we finally hung up.

I stared at my cellphone and, rising from my bed, I walked to the window. I noticed that the rain had stopped by then. I was tired and hungry, so I picked up an apple from the kitchen and, munching on it, I lay down on my bed. Then I went over our conversation again, over all that had happened, every detail . . . I don't know when I fell asleep and started dreaming . . .

The next morning was beautiful, with the sunrays bouncing into my room through the window. The mornings after a rainy night are really pleasant. With my eyes partially open, I smiled to myself, recalling the previous night. I managed to pull myself up, sat on the bed and turned to see myself in the mirror, still smiling. Then I asked my reflection, 'Still in her hangover, *haan*?'

And what a night it was. If a hypothetical kiss could give so much a pleasure, what would a practical one be like, I wondered. Then I decided to call her up—to tease her for all she ended up doing the night before.

She picked up the phone in her sleep and asked, '*Mera baby uth gaya?*'

'Aah . . . You kill me when you talk so sweet.'

'Really?'

'Hmm . . .'

'But I am still sleepy and want to return to my dreams again,' she said.

Mischievously, I shouted at her, 'Sleep? I am here to wake you up! Do you even remember what all you said to a guy last night? I mean, I wonder how you could be so open and bold, forcing me to say all that. You know, I was struggling to get over the embarrassment. I never thought you would cross all the boundaries of shyness, ethical values . . .'

I had not yet finished my speech when she woke up completely and shouted back at me, '*Aaye-haye . . . haye . . .* You guys! How cunning you are, my God! All you boys are alike. The lines you said just now should be mine actually. You stole my lines just because I was sleepy. You crossed all your boundaries and pulled me to the other side as well. How could you do that? You guys play so smart with innocent girls like me . . .'

'Hey,' I said, interrupting, trying to calm her down. But she kept going like an opposition party's representative on NDTV's Big Fight.

'. . . All you guys are like chameleons, changing your colour when required . . . You . . .'

And I was trying to recall where I had heard about chameleons.

Probably in Biology. Was it some kind of flower which changed colour at night and returned to its original colour in the morning? I think it was something else. I wasn't that good with Bio.

Keeping the chameleon at bay, I tried to interrupt again, '*Achcha baba*, listen to me.'

'. . . And only you boys want to talk like this, we girls never . . .' She was not through yet.

'Hey, Khushi . . .' I said, but she was completely ignoring me. '. . . And you know what? All you boys . . .'

'OK ENOUGH!' I shouted, 'YOU KNOW WHAT? THAT HALF AN HOUR LAST NIGHT IS SO PRECIOUS TO ME, THAT I AM READY TO DIE A HUNDRED DEATHS TO ENJOY THAT AGAIN WITH YOU . . . AND JUST YOU.' This time, she heard every word loud and clear. I continued, 'Because it was so sweet, so loving, and so beautiful. And I am so happy that you trust me enough to allow me to get so close to you. And I want to say that . . . I love you so much.'

And she melted like an ice-cream in summer.

'*Sachhi*?' Her innocent, sweet voice was calm now.

'*Muchhi*. I will wait for our engagement evening to come true this way. Just make sure that you don't put on a lot of lipstick.'

'Shut up,' she said shyly.

All day I waited for the confirmation of news which would have been good, if it had been at another time. Unfortunately, I got the confirmation and I had to tell her and my family too. I wondered if she would be happy when she found out, or sad.

Still, without thinking any further, I called her up to tell her. When she did not pick her phone, I got back to my studies. Five minutes later, I heard my cellphone ringing. I could see her name flashing on the screen.

I picked up the phone and said, 'Hi, *Jaaaaaaaaaan*,' very romantically, with a small kiss.

'Uh . . . Hi.'

Damn! It was Neeru, her younger sister. What a blunder. What should I say now? Should I talk or should I just disconnect? I was panicking. With the kind of image I had projected to her family, that first line would have been a shock for sure.

'How are you?' Neeru asked me, breaking the silence.

'Uh . . . I am fine. How are you? And how come you called up from her cell,' I asked, scratching my head and wondering whether she hadn't heard my previous line because of some *chamatkaar* or due to some fault in the phone or the network.

'I am fine. Actually, Khushi was in the washroom and I was about to take your call when the ring stopped. So I dialed the missed-call number. Well, here she is, back in this room. And now she is struggling with me to snatch her cellphone . . .' and her voice faded into the background.

Finally, Khushi said, '*Haan* . . . Hello,' defending herself from her sister's punches. Neeru wanted to talk to me, and it was probably the only time when I felt uncomfortable talking to her, just because of the way the call started.

'Hey, thank God you came,' I said to her.

'Shona, *ek minute*,' she paused with that sentence to hear something which Neeru was trying to tell her at the other end. That '*ek minute*' lasted for five minutes and I realized how wrong I was to think of any *chamatkaar*.

'What?' Khushi shouted, amused, and laughed crazily.

'Hi, *meri jaan*!' Neeru shouted from behind and joined her sister's laughter.

'OH MY GOD!' I thought, feeling very embarrassed.

But Khushi didn't come to my defence. Rather, she joined her sister in celebrating that moment.

'Damn!' I thought. 'Her little sister talked to me as if she didn't hear anything and look at her now. Girls!' I now remembered what a chameleon was, and thought the analogy suited girls even better—they change colours so fast.

So that was how I became a joke for the two sisters.

I almost forgot the reason I had called her, when Khushi came back at last, taking a break from her laughter.

'Yeah . . . Tell me now. She's gone to another room.'

'Your sister is so cunning. She behaved as if she did not hear anything.'

'After all, she's my sister!'

'Now I won't be able to face her for the next few days.'

'Oh come on! After all you are her jiju, and such things keep happening between jiju and saali.'

'But, the next time, I won't begin with romantic lines, unless I make sure it's you on phone.'

'Ok *baba*, now tell me. What were you going to say?'

After a small pause, I said in a single go, 'I need to go to the US for four weeks, for my project.'

'What?' Actually it was more like, 'W-H-A-T?????' A single word with a thousand thoughts running through it, all in different directions.

'Yes.'

'Why so suddenly?' she asked impatiently.

'I knew that this thing was in the pipeline. But I was trying to avert it for the CAT in November. There isn't any escape from this now.'

'But . . . you can make any high priority excuse, right?'

'Hmm . . . But it's going to matter for my career too, dear. Listen. Please don't get angry. At this point, I am a little confused about how I will do this. I mean, leaving the IMS classes, the mock-tests. I need your support.'

'IMS, mock-tests, career . . . You remember everything, but what about me? Busy in our office, career and IMS classes, we have not even seen each other yet. Ours is such a different story . . . And now you're saying you are going to the States . . .' She was about to cry.

'Hey . . . But I have something to cheer you up.'

'What is it?'

'I will be boarding my plane from New Delhi. I'll take a day's leave so that I can spend an entire day with you. We'll finally be seeing each other! Isn't that something to cheer up about?'

Even I knew that it wasn't the perfect way to cheer her up—spending an entire day with her and then leaving the country for more than a month. But the fact that we would get to spend an entire day with each other gave some comfort to our hearts. It was not as if we had any option other than eagerly waiting for that day to arrive and then trying to make it last as long as a year.

What was surprising, though, was that an official, on-site trip was giving us the opportunity to see each other for the very first time. At times, we wondered how busy our life was: running from office to IMS, from career to family, but with no time to see the person with whom we were going to spend the rest of our lives.

Every passing day was marked. And as time passed, our feelings got stronger. The excitement was increasing, both, in the mind and in the heart. And finally, the day arrived when we met each other for the very first time.

~

It is a hot, sticky Sunday afternoon. We are watching the same movie on our televisions: she, in Faridabad; I, in Bhubaneswar. And I am doing this because she sent me an SMS, telling me to watch it.

In the movie, the heroine is packing her bags after having a big fight with her hubby.

At this very moment, Khushi calls me up. And putting herself in that woman's shoes, I don't understand why, she says, 'You know what? If someday I am so angry that I want to run away from you . . . just do a simple thing . . .'

I don't say anything, but she continues.

'Simply run to me and give me a tight hug, no matter how much I hit you then. But give me a warm, tight hug. Don't say a word. Just hold me in your arms for sometime . . . And, a little later, help me in unpacking my bags. Bolo karoge na?'

Face-to-Face

It was 2.30 in the afternoon and I was on an airbus from Bhubaneswar to Delhi. First row, window seat. I just love getting window seats.

With my official laptop on my lap, I wasn't working extra hours and making Infy proud of me. Rather, I was going through her pictures which I'd managed to download at the very last minute before leaving for the airport.

During the journey, I gave plenty of reasons to the air hostesses and my fellow passengers to think that there was something wrong with me. Or, to be precise, with my brain. When you see a guy talking to his laptop, at times looking outside at the clouds, smiling, then looking at the screen again and smiling one more time—you cannot be blamed for feeling that his top floor might be vacant.

I remember the discomfort of the air hostess when she caught me smiling at my laptop while she was delivering the safety demo. She probably hated me because the demo was supposed to be in sync with the announcement by her colleague, and she was lagging behind. But who asked her to focus on me? I didn't.

On my computer screen
Gazing at her picture

I found myself falling with the rising heights
Falling in Love with her
Couldn't resist saying—I love you
The madness added
When the picture said it too

If you ask me why I was blushing and smiling, I had plenty of answers for that. Enjoying the candies (served by the same air hostess), I was recalling how Khushi gave me a call last night as the minute hand just moved past 12 a.m. and we entered the first minute of a new day—today.

'You are going to come to me todayyyyy,' she shouted

'Oh Boy! I am going crazzzyyyyyyyy,' I also shouted, jumping in my balcony, stirring the calm midnight.

I guess I woke up some of my neighbors, and disturbed some who were about to orgasm. A couple of street dogs came out of the darkness and started barking at me. I rushed back into my room when I saw the lights turn on in a few flats in the building next to mine.

Laughing at last night's events and still enjoying my candies, I recollected how confused I was that morning about what to wear. I pulled out everything from my closet that morning and tried it all in front of the mirror. I took almost an hour to decide and, then, changed again just before I left for the office. The funny thing is that I ended up wearing the only shirt which wasn't ironed (along with dark denim).

Everything I did that day, I made a mess of. And while I recalled those moments, every now and then weird thoughts would pop into my head—

What if she isn't as beautiful as she appears in her pictures?
What if she laughs in a very weird way?
What if she limps?

—and many other such thoughts played hide and seek in my mind, until I finally asked myself the big question.

Do you love her, Ravin?

Holy shit! Of course it was too late to be asking this.

'Yes, I do. Of course I do,' I said to myself.

Well, to be honest, I actually forced myself to say it. I don't know why I was a little apprehensive. But, good or bad, the truth was that marrying her was my independent decision, one that I had arrived at without any kind of pressure from my family or from her.

So, to silence those weird thoughts, I pulled out a newspaper from the small rack in front of my seat. But I could not concentrate on the newspaper either. There was a different kind of excitement in me which was sending up a chill inside me, shaking me a bit at times. I don't know what kind of fear it was.

The nervousness and anxiety meant I was going to the loo every twenty minutes. I became a peeing machine. It happens to everyone . . . Or doesn't it? And I was sure that the kid on the last seat was counting the number of times I passed by him. I pretended to ignore him when he started whispering in his mom's ear. Of course he was telling her about me. I noticed his hand pointing at me, which his mom pulled back, smiling.

Finally at 5 in the evening, the plane landed at Delhi and I switched on my mobile completely ignoring the captain's command to not do so before instructed. While the plane was taking a U—turn on the runway, I looked out of the window to see if there was any girl waving towards my plane—it could be her! (Now, I wonder how I could have been so silly as to expect visitors on the runway.)

I was trying to call her up but, for some reason, my cellphone could not adapt itself to the roaming zone. I kept trying, cursing my phone and the network. I kept trying and kept failing.

A few minutes later, I was standing at the baggage claim section, waiting for my luggage to arrive. But my eyes were not on the conveyor belt. They were looking for something else, rather *someone* else. Here and there, I was looking at every girl, and peering at the crowd standing outside which was visible through the glass wall.

Then I saw my red bag gliding towards me on the belt. But before it could reach me, she reached me.

On my phone.

My cell was working now and I heard the ring. 'Khushi calling,' it said. I took her call.

'Hey.'

'Hey.'

Silence.

'So.' And I turned back, facing the exit.

'So.'

'What so?'

'I mean, where are you?'

She had never seemed so shy and silent. I could almost hear her blushing. Obviously, her state of mind was no different from mine. And how could it be? Two people, who were madly in love with each other and had decided to marry each other, were going to see each other for the first time in their life!

'I am at the baggage claim section,' I said. And, with that, I noticed my bag going away from me. 'Damn! I missed it.'

'What did you miss?'

'My luggage. I started talking to you and I missed it.'

'Uh-oh.' She paused while I kept my eyes on the conveyor belt. Then she spoke again, 'Can I ask you something?'

'What?'

'Are you nervous?'

'How do you know?'

'Because . . . even I am,' she confessed. Then she said, 'Ok! Tell me, what are you wearing today?'

'Olive-green shirt and dark-blue jeans. You?'

'Oh my God!'

'What happened?' I thought she didn't like the colour I was wearing.

'It looks good on me.'

'No, no. It's not about good or bad.'

'Then?'

'I am also wearing olive-green and blue jeans.'

Coincidences seemed always to be following us. Our birthplace, the month, the year, our interest in music, our career, IMS. And now, the clothes we were wearing that day.

'Amazing! We are definitely made for each other. Hey! My luggage is coming to me again. I'm going to pick it up and come outside in two minutes. See ya!'

I made my way through the broken queue to get my bag, and loading it on a trolley, I walked towards the exit. The laptop was still hanging on my shoulder.

Finally about to see her, I was anxious, shivering and my heart was beating fast. Every feminine voice from the crowd seemed to be hers. Of course, I was trying to behave as if I was relaxed and cool.

'Relax . . . Relax . . . Relax. Take a deep breath,' I told myself. And the next thing I know, I was already outside.

There were a lot of people in front of me, waiting for their dear ones. Some cab drivers, holding up nameplates for their bosses. There was a lot of shouting and noise from the traffic.

Then, for some reason, I stopped moving forward and turned left.

And there she was!

My angel, my beautiful one.

Her smile which tried to override my senses. That chilling hesitation in her, and in me. Her long, untied hair that fell upon her eyes with a gust of wind. Her hand moving across her face, and moving her hair behind her left ear. Her left ear, and the glittering silver earring she was wearing. Her beautiful face, which mesmerized me. And in that green, off-shoulder top and jeans, her body appeared so perfect, so young, so poised. She was charismatic. I wasn't able to take my eyes off her. Rather, I wanted to stare at her from top to bottom, very slowly—which I actually did.

'This is her,' I told myself. 'She is mine.'

That was a wonderful moment which I have re-lived again and again, recalling that first sight.

I moved towards her with a smile, almost forgetting my trolley. And in a few seconds, there I was, right in front of her, a foot apart, still not able to take my gaze off her.

'Hey,' I said, offering my right hand for a shake.

'Hi,' she responded, politely and in such an elegant way, touching me for the first time with that hand shake. (Did you hear what I said? The first time we touched . . . It was magical!)

And her eyes . . . So beautiful! There was something special in them. Something which didn't let me look away. I wanted to hear what they were telling me. The feeling, the truth of the moment, the . . . the . . . I don't know what it was.

I looked, and my eyes were stuck on you
I tried to move the black in them, but they were stuck like glue

Looking at you for real, I noticed your eyes
That's exactly where your entire beauty lies
So genuine, so honest, so beautiful, so deep
With a glint of light, some naughtiness did creep

Finding my dream coming true
I pleaded my shivering lips to bring out the words I had kept for you

There were so many things to say
I can remember none of them at all
But, I don't lose with that, I do things my own way . . .

'. . . And this is my sister Neeru and he is Girish—her best and only friend,' she broke my gaze and thoughts to introduce me to two other people. I wondered how I didn't notice them standing beside us. Was I so lost in her? Undoubtedly, I was.

I said hello to both of them, cracking some jokes to ease the sweet pressure which Khushi and I were feeling. Then we moved out of the exit channel towards the parking lot in search of the cab these guys had come to the airport in. Khushi was too shy to walk with me and she joined Neeru and Girish in looking for the cab. I followed at a distance, with my trolley. My condition was no different from her.

I wrote her a very short SMS, then, 'You are damn hot!'

The next moment I saw her coming towards me from the other side of the exit, looking at something on her cellphone, probably reading my SMS.

When she reached me, she smiled.

'Thanks,' she said.

'I love this. Whatever is happening. The excitement, the anxiety. And seeing you,' I said.

And in her shyness, she turned away, her hair falling across her eyes again. Her complete attention was upon me, yet she was trying to escape my gaze.

'Hey. Am I making sense? Or am I being stupid?' I asked.

She laughed and turned back to me. She had a lot of teeth. 'No you're making sense, actually. It's the same with me,' she said, smiling.

Soon, Neeru and Girish appeared, pointing at the cab which was coming towards us. It became clear that I was expected to step into the cab first, and because of this I panicked.

Where should I sit? I asked myself. In the back, with her? But will it look good if I sit between the two sisters, pushing Girish to the front? Should I sit in front, then? Or should I sit in the back, but on the left, with Girish in middle and Khushi at the right. And her sister with the driver? No. No. What a mess! So many permutations and combinations to be solved in a second. It was beyond the abilities of my brain. Better sit up front, I thought. It was the easiest solution.

And in haste and alarm I got in beside the driver. 'You fool. What is she going to think of you? Why didn't you sit behind, beside her?' my not-so-talented brain shouted at me the very next second. Damn! I was screwing up things with my stupidity. I was sitting apart from my own girlfriend.

Barely a minute later, I got a call on my cell. Mom calling.

'Shit! She asked me to call her the moment I landed in Delhi. I forgot,' I murmured as I took the call. '*Haanji* Mumma, I just came out of the airport,' I said before she asked me anything.

'I knew you will forget. Now tell me,' she said

'Tell me? What?' I asked, though I knew she probably had a hundred questions for me, about Khushi, which I couldn't answer because I was with them in the cab.

But she didn't ask me all those questions. Just one, which summarized all of them, 'So, are you happy?'

'Oh Mom! I am . . . I am very happy,' I replied quietly, looking outside the window.

'Good. I just wanted to know that. I know you won't want to talk to me at this moment. So you guys enjoy and we will talk later. All right?'

'*Haanji* Mumma, *theek hai*. I will call you later. Bye.'

We were now on our way to the hotel, which I was to move into for slightly more than a day before I left for the US. I had no idea where this hotel was, nor did the cab driver. Khushi and Girish said they did but both were pointing in opposite directions. In other words no one had a clue. But we moved ahead thinking we'd soon ask somebody about the precise location.

What an evening that was! I was sitting beside the driver and behind me was my sweetheart, with Neeru in the middle and Girish on her right. The song selection on the radio seemed to be exceptionally good that day—romantic songs that Khushi and I could relate to—and we sat listening to them without saying anything, but smiling within.

These moments of silence only added to the beauty of the songs. I tried to see her in the rearview mirror but, every time, I'd only find Girish's funny face and he would raise his eyebrows, mocking me.

Soon, however, our formal demeanor gave way to a more casual one and we started talking about each other, at times pulling each other's leg, recalling some stupid incidents out of the blue and spicing them up as we narrated them. Khushi became an easy target for both Neeru and Girish and they mimicked her embarrassment that day, before seeing me. We were shouting and partying in the cab with the patties and the pastries they had brought.

'*Yeh lo, ladki vaalon ki taraf se,*' Girish said offering me the box of pastries.

We were in a jolly mood and, adding to the delight, it started drizzling outside. Shouting, laughing, going crazy to those peppy numbers, we were having a gala time in the cab. On a few occasions, secretly, she pinched me from behind, and I just loved that.

For more than an hour and a half, we hunted for my hotel on the streets of Delhi. And, more than anybody (even me), Khushi was concerned about this. According to her, I was tired from my journey and needed some rest, but I wondered why I didn't feel that way.

It was around 7.30 in the evening when we finally reached the Qutub Din hotel, in the vicinity of the Qutub Minar, thanks to the chaiwalas and paanwalas. We all entered the hotel and, at the reception, I checked out my booking.

'Room no. 301. That way, sir. The boy will bring your luggage in,' said a man with a huge moustache, at the reception counter.

'All right,' I said and we all headed towards 301, everyone following me.

Neeru and Girish were talking to each other in whispers when Khushi said something to me, very politely

'Can you walk a little slower? You've left me behind.'

And I realized why people say that girls are far more mature than guys. I was a fool, earlier, leaving her on the backseat of the cab and taking the front one. And here, again, I was walking alone, leaving her behind. I started panicking, not knowing how to handle such situations. I was a boyfriend for the first time. A fresher in the school of romance.

'God! Please help me,' I muttered and decelerated.

She came closer to me and said, 'Now you're not alone. You have a girl in your life. So walk beside her.'

Behind us, Neeru and Girish smiled naughtily.

'Won't they leave us alone for a while?' I thought. But how could they hear my thoughts? They kept following us.

We were at 301. I opened the door to my room and we all went in.

The room was well lit. A small table, with a telephone and a flower vase, separating the two beds. Nice bed-sheets. There was a telephone directory and a menu beside the TV set, across from the beds. A giant mirror on the wall in front of us which reflected the entire room, including those two beds and a cupboard near the entrance. Beside the mirror, there was a door to the washroom.

'Hmm . . . This is good,' I announced.

'Yeah', 'Yup', 'Hmm . . .' the people surrounding me murmured. Then, Girish started his survey of the room, analysing everything and telling me the good and the bad.

'Thanks Girish,' I said, when he had finished. 'Anytime,' he acknowledged.

After which I wanted to ask him just one more question—'So when are you going to leave us alone, for heaven's sake!?' Instead, I just kept mum, hoping my eyes would do the talking. And Neeru finally understood that they should better leave us alone for a while. She whispered to Girish and I don't know what was making the three of them look at each other and smile. I hoped they were not joking about me.

'We are going to a nearby place to have something. If you guys want, we can get something for you,' Girish said, moving towards the door with Neeru.

'No. I'm stuffed,' I said. 'Wow! At last,' I thought.

'Girish, if we need something, I will call you up. And take care of Neeru. Don't leave her alone, all right?' Khushi said, opening the Bisleri bottle placed on the table.

'Yes, I will. You don't worry. By the way, it's 8.30 now. We should leave Delhi by 9 so that we can reach Faridabad by about 10.15.

We're already late, you know *na*?'

'Yeah. But don't worry, we will manage,' said Khushi.

'All right. See ya.'

And finally they left the room and I took a deep breath to relax.

I went and locked the door while Khushi took a last sip of water from the bottle. She noticed me doing that and smiled, then she kept the bottle on the table and my laptop bag on the chair. I stepped between the two beds and sat on the left one. She came in and sat on the right one, just in front of me. We were together, just the two of us. Our smiles described our mood.

That moment seemed to be a beautiful dream. We wanted to feel and live that moment forever. The person with whom I was going to spend the rest of my life was right in front of me. I could look into her beautiful eyes, I could touch her, feel her. The delight of that moment had both of us spellbound. Words were unnecessary. I stared at her for a long time. And when she could not handle my gaze, she looked at the ground, her neck tilting down and strands of her beautiful hair falling in front of her shoulder, covering her right cheek and ear.

And the silence in the room persisted, and there we were, madly in love. Still not believing that, finally, we had seen each other. Still nervous, still wondering what to say.

Gathering her courage, she looked up, into my eyes (which were still focused on her) and moving her hair behind her ear again, she asked, '*Safar mein koi takleef to nahi hui*?'

Coming as it did, after more than five minutes of silence, that question sounded hilarious. It reminded us both of the old Bollywood movies in which the heroine would ask her beloved, '*Suniye ji, aapke safar mein . . .*' and all that. Before she could see my reaction, she understood what a stupid and stereotypical question it was, and we looked at each other and laughed and laughed, falling upon our respective beds. But that question also became an ice breaker and we both relaxed.

'Ha ha ha ha! Yeah, I mean, *nahi koi takleef nahi hui,*' I said, getting up.

'I am so stupid,' she said, slapping her forehead.

'Nah, you're not. You are . . . beautiful,' I said calmly, looking into her eyes.

And I don't know what gave me the courage to raise my right hand towards her, to reach her face. My fingers first touched her cheek, the middle finger first, then the first finger and then all of them, helping her hair behind her ear. That human touch was incredible. Feeling my fingers on her face, she closed her eyes and I felt her breathing heavily now. I watched her. Her good-looking face, the lines on her forehead, appearing and vanishing. Her curved eyelashes. Her cute nose. Her soft lips, which I very gently rubbed my thumb on, and she started shaking, her eyes still closed and her hands gripping the bed-sheet very tight. My eyes were the silent observers to this moment we both were in. My mind was hypnotized and fingers were still trying to understand the beautiful face before me. Occasionally, I felt her warm breath breaking on my cold fingers.

My consciousness asked me whether what was happening was real and then it answered itself—I was not dreaming. She was real. She was with me. Deep inside, I felt so satisfied, so blessed that the moment when my angel was in front of me had finally arrived.

We were lost. Lost in each other.

'Shonimoni,' I whispered in her ears, silently, getting close to her, very close. She was still breathing heavily and couldn't say anything. 'This is a wonderful moment. I can't believe this. You are with me . . .'

I moved almost to her bed.

'Shona!' she said and grabbed my hand.

In a while, very slowly, she opened her eyes and looked at me and smiled. She was so happy, so delighted to have me so close to her. And she kept looking at me in that way, for some time.

Raising her eyebrows slightly and still smiling, she asked me, 'Tell me, how you are feeling at this instant, with me?'

I put my arms around her and biting her ear, I said, 'Don't ask me. I won't be able to describe it. I just want to say one thing . . .' Then, I whispered in her ear, 'I am madly in love with you.' With that, I rested my chin on her shoulder.

'I love you too,' she said and moved her fingers all the way from my forearms, to the wrist, then the palm and finally into the spaces between my fingers. At that moment, I felt so complete. I realized how, just like me, she too wanted to live that moment as if it should never end.

I held her in my arms for some time. From the romantic movies I had seen till then, I knew that holding your beloved in your arms that way is such a different feeling. But that it would be so magical, I never knew. To understand and believe certain things, you have to experience them. And love is one such thing. Hmmm . . . Actually, it's not a thing—it's a lot more than that. We were speechless again, just feeling each other. But who needed to talk? Silence was talking at its best. But threatening the silence, another thought crept into my heart, all of a sudden . . . Should I kiss her? And, with that, the battle between my heart and mind started. Heart: Yes. Mind: No. Heart: Why not? This is such a perfect moment. I think I should. Mind: What if she doesn't feel good about it? After all, this is just your first date. Heart: But will I get a moment like this again? Tomorrow, her entire family will be around us. No time, then. And the next day I have to take my flight. I should take a chance right now . . . Mind: Chance? First, look into the mirror and ask yourself if you can do this in the first day itself? Heart: Stop that nonsense. I am going ahead. Mind: Good luck. Heart: Thanks . . . Mind: Hey wait a sec. Heart: Now what?

Mind: Are you comfortable? May be you want to use the loo first . . . It helps, you know.

Heart: Shut up! Now, this happens to me most of the time. Sometimes, I think, I am not too strong, mentally. And that's why my heart always wins. But, to be very honest, I just love that.

I oxygenated my lungs with a deep breath and turned her almost 180 degrees. We now were facing each other. My arms were still around her, her hands were on my shoulders. I looked into her eyes.

> *I grabbed her*
> *Looked straight into her eyes*
> *I told her, I do things*
> *And I do them in my own way.*

I was prepared to feel something for the very first time in my life and—I won't lie—my heartbeats, at that moment, were faster than Schumacher in his Ferrari. I looked into her eyes and drew close.

> *I grabbed her*
> *Looked straight into her eyes*
> *With a wink, I drew her close*
> *My lips moved, but this time not to say*
>
> *I told her, I do things*
> *And I do them in my own way.*

Yes, it was going to be my first ever kiss . . .

But!

But . . . How I hate to the word B-U-T.

But fate had to intervene and Girish, playing devil, called her up on her cell. The ringtone shattered my utopia and, before I could reach her lips, she wanted to answer the call. And before she could answer the call, she looked at the clock.

'Oh my God! It's 9! N-I-N-E!' she said, (no, she screamed) and stretched to reach her cellphone.

'It's Girish,' she said, pressing the answer button.

While she was talking to Girish, I collapsed on the bed in total dismay, wondering at Girish's sense of timing. How could he be so perfect? I was fuming inside.

All the while, she continued with that call:

'*Haan bolo.*'

'Yeah, I know we have to leave.' She turned her back to me and walked towards the door which was locked from inside.

'No, we don't want anything to eat.' She looked back at me and gestured with her other hand to ask me if I was hungry.

'Yes Girish, just five more minutes *yaar*.' She clenched and unclenched her fist.

'*Arey*, I know *baba*. I said *na*, we will manage,' and she looked at herself in the mirror.

'Now will you please hang up? Pleaseeeee?' She turned her back towards the mirror.

'Yeah, we will be there in five minutes. All right? Bye now.' And she came to me, disconnecting the call. She was panicking, all of a sudden.

'Shona! I have to leave. I am getting late. Mom must be about to call.'

'Hmm . . . All right. Don't worry, you'll be on time. Where are Neeru and Girish?' I tried to comfort her and, more importantly, to extinguish the fire that had just now been burning in me.

'At the reception,' she answered.

'Ok. And I guess you guys will be going by the same cab,' I asked, getting up from the bed and taking a sip of water from the half-filled bottle.

'Yes, the same cab,' she said, getting up and moving towards the mirror again.

Then her cellphone rang again and, again, it was Girish. I picked up the call this time.

'Hey, I guess you should hurry up. It has started raining again,' he said.

Though I hated him at that moment, I still said, 'Yes, just a second. We are coming down. See you there.'

We were about to leave that room, when she screamed one

more time. 'Shit! I forgot this,' she said, looking at the big plastic bags which Neeru had left at the entrance to the room.

She quickly picked them up and said, 'Shona, this is for you.'

'What is this?'

'Open it.'

I did what she asked. A blue-striped shirt with a Park Avenue tag and two ties: one, black with white stripes in the middle; the other, steel-coloured. I was so pleased. A girl bought something for me . . . My Khushi bought something for me. And I suddenly recalled a couple of managers from my office whom I used to see, at times, in shops along with their wives, who were selecting shirts for them. I felt good, realizing all those things were happening to me now. New things, different things, beautiful things.

'For me?' I asked her. 'No. For that fat cab driver,' she tried to tease me. 'Really? You had an affair with him too?' I teased her back. 'Shut up,' she responded with a smile but her eyes wanted me to fear her. Then she reminded me, 'I have to rush now. It has started raining.'

'Oh yes. Let's go,' I said, dropping the box on the bed behind me and stepping out of the room. This time I made sure to walk beside her, and she acknowledged that with her mischievous smile.

We were about to reach the reception when I couldn't control myself any more and asked her, 'Why are you leaving Khushi? Don't go . . . Please.' And my speech paused there, along with my feet.

She stopped there as well and held my hand in hers and said, 'Just a couple of months and I won't have to leave you this way. I will be all yours.' There was so much love in those words as if, from now on, she was going to take care of me forever.

'I know,' I said.

'Now shall we go before Girish gives another call?'

'Yes.'

Back at the reception, we met Neeru and Girish again. They were trying to tease Khushi with their faces and expressions but she was, somehow, managing everything with her simple smiles, digressing from what they wanted to hear. We all stood there for a few minutes before they went to their cab which was parked outside the hotel.

It was drizzling. They got seated and the cab reversed. They were leaving and my eyes were following the left window from which she was waving to me. I almost ran into the middle of the road to catch a last glimpse of her for the day. Then the cab took a right turn at the end of the street and she disappeared.

But Oh! I loved the light rain shower and looked up at the sky, thanking the heavenly firmament.

That day did not end there, though.

A few minutes later, I was in my room, busy performing my victory dance and singing the lines '*pehla nasha, pehla khumaar.*' Just like in the movie, I placed my left foot on the bed and jumped back on the ground to my right, in slow motion. The only difference being, my landing was not successful and I broke the glass of water placed beside the TV.

Shattered glass on the floor. And silence . . .

Standing alone, in front of the mirror I scolded my reflection, 'See what you have done?'

The very next moment, my reflection smiled and murmured, '*naya pyaar hai, naya imtihaan.*'

I was out of control, wondering how I could tell the world that I was the happiest man on the planet at that moment. The feelings within me were straining to come out. And I don't know whether I was failing to handle them, or celebrating them in the best possible way.

Finally, I grabbed my cell again to give her a call and tell her, 'You are damn beautiful. You are so perfect . . . I am so lucky . . .' I went on and on, and she heard all that with a smile.

She was still in that cab and I could hear giggling voices around her. All she said was, 'And vice versa. I have so much to say, but just can't. You know *na*.'

We talked for a very short while and then I ordered my dinner which arrived in another ten minutes. By 10.30, I had eaten and the bellboy came to my room to collect the dinner plates and bowls.

'How was the food, sir?' he asked.

Did I really notice the taste? Forget the taste, did I even know what dishes I had eaten? All I could think of was her face, the way it appeared when I pulled her in my arms, her eyes and her fragrance which still persisted in my breath.

But I answered, 'Oh yes, it was good.'

He gathered the plates and left my room.

By 11.30, I still couldn't sleep, though I was tired. I was hung over on something so different, for the first time. I was celebrating the spirit of being in love. Everything around me appeared beautiful because the only thing running through my mind was beautiful.

She too was going through something similar, I learnt when she called me at last. And we talked for a long time, candidly: confessing our fears; describing the thoughts flowing in our mind when we saw each other at the airport, when I sat on the front seat, leaving her behind, when I locked the door of my room from inside once Neeru and Girish had left, when I pulled her in my arms; our happiness, the euphoria in which we still were. I don't remember when, exactly, we slept . . .

The next morning, I was waiting for Girish. Khushi had called me up to tell me that Girish would be coming to Delhi for some work and would pick me up on his way back to Faridabad. There, for the first time, I'd meet Khushi's family—except for her dad who was in Punjab, taking part in some religious event at a *gurudwara* there.

While I waited for him, I spent my time doing some peculiar things. Standing in front of the mirror, I practiced lines which I might have to say in front of her family in different situations. I wanted my facial expressions and body language to make a good impression on her family. So, I rehearsed some common lines:

'No, no, my parents won't have any issues if she carries on with her career after marriage. In fact, I am marrying her because she is a career-oriented girl.' (With a brilliant use of the hands.)

'I'm not sure if we'll move north so soon but, yes, the plans are there.' (With confidence.)

'Oh yes, I can cook. In my work-related trips abroad I learnt that, you know. It might not be as delicious as what she can prepare, but it serves its purpose.' (With a smile.)

And so on.

It was 10 a.m. To kill some more time, I moved out to the lounge. I was nervous again as I left my room. The nervousness of facing so many new people at once. In the lounge, I glanced through the newspaper and had a cup of tea, which was my only breakfast. I wasn't feeling hungry at all, but excited and thrilled.

A few minutes later, my cellphone beeped. It was an SMS from her.

Girish wl b dere by 10.15.
B ready and Gud Luk. A few
hrs from now u'll b among
ur would be in laws. :-)

As soon as I read her message, a new number flashed on my cell's screen. This time, it was Girish calling me outside. I quickly finished my tea, put the newspaper back in the rack and left the hotel.

Soon, I was in his Qualis. Obviously, his dad was a big man. On our way to Faridabad, he kept telling me about his dad, who had been an MLA some years back. He kept talking about his investments in real estate and in shares. And I kept replying with 'ok,' 'yeah' and 'oh really'—not really listening to his big talk. All that was going through my mind at that point was how things would pan out in the next couple of hours. I had never been to any in-laws till then! With the rest of our relatives, it was always the boy's family who went to the girl's. But here, things were so different. I was all alone. So many thoughts going through my mind . . .

I am all alone. Damn! I don't even believe I am doing this, going to visit my in-laws.

Do I need to tell her mother one more time that I love Khushi?

Thank God her dad is not home.

I should sound mature. A responsible citizen. Shit! Not citizen. A responsible person who will keep their Khushi very happy for the rest of her life.

What will her home be like? Bigger than mine?

Is anybody going to ask me my salary? Should I add a few more thousands to the figure?

They have a big car too and I have just a bike—not even a Pulsar, at that.

Damn! What all I am thinking? Shit!

'What happened?' asked Girish. 'No, no, nothing,' I said, wondering if he heard my thoughts. 'Hey! Hey! *Aisa hi hota hai*,' he mocked my condition. 'What do you mean, *aisa hi hota hai*?' I asked to hide my restlessness. '*Kuch nahin*,' he said with a smile and put on some music. After almost an hour, we reached our destination. On the way, I bought a pineapple cake for them from a confectionary in Faridabad, which Girish said was one of the best in their city. 'Here we are. *Lo aa gaya aapka sasuraal*,' said Girish. 'Boy! This is it,' I said to myself.

I took a deep breath and got down from the vehicle and looked at the white-coloured house in front of me. Then I opened the black gate and walked in. There were a few plants, with flowers blossoming in them. A tiled veranda, half of which was covered with a shed. I knocked on the door in front of me, while Girish came after locking his car.

Somebody opened the door and I was excited to see who it was going to be.

Her mom. In a very simple and decent suit. No makeup at all, simply a *kada* in her right hand. She appeared as simple as my mom. She smiled when she opened the door to welcome me in.

'*Sat Sri Akal*,' I said and bent down to touch her feet.

'*Sat Sri Akal beta ji*,' she said kissing my forehead.

Her mom was delighted to see me. Finally, I was in front of her eyes. She was seeing, for the first time, the person who was going to take her beloved daughter away from her. And in those eyes were so many expectations, so many concerns and so much hope for her daughter.

She welcomed me into the drawing room. Girish followed me, touching her feet.

'*Baitho beta*,' she said to both of us.

While we made ourselves comfortable, she asked me if I was well and if my journey had been comfortable. Then she went out of the room, saying '*Main bas abhi aayi*.' Probably, she went to the kitchen.

Back in the drawing room, I was adapting to my would-be *sasuraal*. I liked the ambience of the room: the sofa and the chairs surrounding the center-table at one end of the room; the TV set at the opposite end, in a movable cabinet that had a lot of other stuff on its shelves decorative pieces, including small, flowery miniatures on the upper left, a toy-train on the right (possibly Daan's); the money-plant in one corner, between the sofas and chairs; a couple of beautiful paintings on the wall with the signatures of their makers at the bottom-right. The one in front of me was big, almost a meter long, and depicted the *baaraat* of a Prince, who was on his horse, with his bride being carried in a *doli* and a few people playing the *shehnai*.

'How are you feeling?' Girish whispered from the other end of the sofa, having his share of fun in all that was happening.

'I am doing fine,' I whispered back.

'Good,' he smiled.

A little later, somebody came into the room. A beautiful girl in alight green top and black denim, with a tray in her hand, carrying soft-drinks in beautifully carved glasses. It was Neeru. The day before, I had not noticed how beautiful she was. But how could I, when her still more beautiful sister was in front of me. Anyway, I was happy with one more thought, 'Beautiful *Saali* too.'

So, this is how it started. With cold drinks and a whole lot of snacks, dry fruits and sweets. Neeru and her mom joining us with their chitchat. Questions from her mom: How was my family doing back in Orissa? For how long was I going abroad? And many more . . . At times, she talked about their family, which means that I got to know once more, the things I already knew.

Deepu was in Assam, working with an MNC. Pushkar and Amrit (a.k.a. Ami di) would be here in half an hour or so.

Already, there were so many similarities between Khushi and me. And, now, I saw so many similarities between our families too. Both were religious-minded and believed in simple living. Her mother, in each and every aspect, appeared just like my mother.

As we talked, I occasionally kept raising my eyebrows looking at Neeru, silently asking her about her elder sister's whereabouts.

'Have patience. She is getting ready. *Sirf aapke liye hi,*' she replied and laughed at me. Then she brought me a plate, 'Take one *samosa.*'

'*Haanji beta, lo na,*' her mom insisted.

And this continued

'Oh! Have some cashews.'

'Thanks.'

'Try this *aloo bhujia.*'

'No, please. I'm stuffed.'

'No, no . . . Take some. All right, try this *dhokla* then. You will love it.'

'A . . . a . . . all right. But this is the last one.'

'*Arey, aap to kuch le hi nahi rahe ho . . . Yeh lo na.*'

'*Nahin,* please. Thanks. *Bas, bas, bas!* This is too much . . .'

With so much, I feared constipation and, if not that, definitely loose motions.

Almost twenty minutes passed and there was still no sign of the girl I had come there for. Back in that room, the four of us were talking to each other. At times, Neeru and Girish were smiling at each other.

Then all of a sudden, a voice traveled from inside, 'Neeeeeruuuuuu!'

'*Lo, ho gai taiyaar maharani,*' Neeru said, getting up from her chair and going to Khushi.

Moments later, I heard two different footsteps approaching us.

There she was. My angel in a ravishing suit: pink *kameez,* sky blue *pyjaami* and a blended *chunni* with many shiny stones making uneven lines on it. Her hair, long and silky. Glossy lips and those glittering ear rings.

She looked at me and said, 'Hi!'

'Hi!' I responded with a smile, amazed at how beautiful she looked.

There was a different kind of hesitation between us now, to talk to each other in front of everybody. Still, we went ahead.

With her eyes she asked how she looked.

And I said, 'You look amazing.'

'Thank you,' she said and joined us.

She sat right in front of me. She really looked so beautiful in Indian-wear. I wished everybody in that house would vanish for a couple of hours, so that I could keep staring at her that way.

We all started talking. Every now and then, she was adjusting her *chunni* which kept sliding down her right shoulder. On her mom's insistence, she picked up a few cashews from the dry-fruits bowl, leaving the *dhokla* and *rasgullas* because they would mess her lipstick. At times, she looked at me and noticed how I was looking at her with everyone around and she silently begged me to take my eyes off her. But men will always be men.

To break her spell on me, she started talking to me.

'What time is your flight tomorrow?'

'7:30 in the morning.'

'So you'll have to leave the hotel at around 4:30, then?'

'Yeah, I have to wake up early tomorrow.'

And we all kept talking for a while. I was much more comfortable by then, apart from the fear of being offered more food. Girish wanted to leave. He had just risen from the couch when we heard a car arriving at the gate.

'Hey! Ami di *aa gayi*,' Neeru almost sang that, rushing to the door and peeping out.

'And Pushkar?' I wanted to confirm the arrival of another male too.

'*Unke saath hi to aayi hongi,*' Girish said.

And few seconds later, both Pushkar and Ami di came in, wiping their shoes on the door-mat. Everyone stood up to welcome them, as if they were the ones for whom we all had assembled. Seeing them, I got up too.

'Wow! Such a warm welcome for the second son-in-law of the house. Hmm . . . I'm the next. Tough competition, dude!' I thought to myself.

In her black top and blue denim, Ami di looked like a professional, 21st century lady. Her denim was in the latest, weird fashion—the one in which girls would fold up their jeans' legs a few inches above their ankles, showing the light, inner colour of the denim. I don't know what's so exciting about it. We guys used to do that while playing soccer in mud, in our school days. Her glasses had a stylish frame, and she had a different style of tying her hair at the back—of course, a modern one.

Altogether, Ami di appeared a 'Yo! Yo!' girl.

A 'Yo! Yo!' girl, in our term means . . . a . . . a . . . Yo! Yo! kind of gal.

The thing which I liked most in her was the red and white bangles covering both her hands. Of course, they revealed that she got married that very year. According to custom, these bangles stayed on the hands of a newly-married girl for almost a year.

Pushkar appeared very simple to me.

After shaking hands and saying 'hi' and 'hello,' everybody settled down on the sofas and chairs. Conversation started again.

'So how are you, Ravin?' Pushkar asked.

'I am fine, thanks. How are you guys doing?' I asked, looking at both of them. 'Pretty good. And how are your parents and brother back there?'

Ami di asked this time.

'They are doing well,' I replied with a smile.

And so we continued our chitchat on various topics: my office, their office, Khushi's office; the different places we visited, which was a chance for me to boast about my trips abroad; Delhi traffic, CAT, the next Indian Idol and what not . . .

And, yes, there was a second round of snacks and, of course, I had to keep the new arrivals company. I felt like I was going to explode.

Meanwhile, Girish got another call on his cell and, the way he rushed out to his Qualis, we were sure it was his dad. All I could say to him was 'thanks'—for helping me reach this place and, more importantly, for being the only other man with me, among those ladies till Pushkar arrived. He left.

The conversation really warmed up in a while, and it didn't take me even half an hour to realize that Pushkar was a cool dude. He appeared to be very practical. And the entire female union kept boasting about his greatest asset—

'*Pata hai, Jiju bahut achcha khaana banaate hain.* He has learnt the art of cooking,' said Neeru proudly, as if her jiju was going to present another cookery show on Star Plus. But, well, a guy who cooks lovely food, knows how to garnish various dishes and how to place the forks and spoons on the dining table is a dream guy for 99.99% of the girls on this planet. (In fact, I'm sure it's the same on other planets too . . . if there are girls on them.)

Neeru had just initiated this topic and it didn't take even a couple of minutes for Pushkar's great hobby to become a threat for me—Khushi's mom threw me a bouncer. '*Beta aap khaana bana lete ho?*' she asked politely and, unfortunately, with much expectation.

Silence. The sound of someone grinding cashew between their teeth could be heard.

Everyone was waiting for my response. It was as if, while following an India-Pakistan cricket match on the radio, they had just heard that

Tendulkar had hit the ball high in the air and were waiting for the commentator to reveal if it was a six or a catch.

Staring at the bubbles in my glass of Coke, I thought, 'Now the next question you will ask me is 'Will you be able to iron her *salwar kameez*?' Or, 'Do you sing? *Arey, kuch gaa ke sunao na*?' See! This is what happens when you come to such places without your parents. The other party tries to validate you on different platforms so candidly, and you cannot say no to every question.'

I tried to come up with some answer, looking at my cellphone and wishing that it would ring so that I could escape the questions which I was going to face. But the damned gadget was meant to ring only at the worst times—like the evening before, with the kiss that could have been—but never when I needed it the most.

Finally, swallowing a few times in my nervousness, I went ahead and told them what they wanted to hear.

'Ah, umm . . . Yes, I can. With most of the things, I am kind of OK. But I make good *paranthas* . . .'

I hadn't even completed, when her sweet and innocent mother, delighted by my answer, asked me, '*Kaun kaun se paranthe*?'

'Now this is too much!' Well, I didn't actually say that, but that's what I was thinking and I wondered if I was supposed to recite a menu list, like Pappu uncle from the Punjabi dhaba at Burla.

But, interestingly, the next moment I had a smile on my face. I was amused at the kind of questions being put to a software engineer. I never thought I'd be facing such an interview, not even in my weirdest dreams. I was happy that, for a change, I was being asked such different questions. I told myself, 'These were not bad questions but exciting ones. Be confident and go ahead.'

And I went ahead and said, 'Mumma, I can prepare many—*aaloo ke, pyaaz ke*, occasionally *gobhi ke* and *mooli ke bhi* in the winters.'

'Wow! Ravin, that's good. When did you learn all this?' Pushkar asked. He seemed to be quite interested.

And I told him, 'When I was in Belgium for eight months. I lived there alone and had to cook for myself. Before that, I never did any cooking. Necessity is the mother of invention, you know . . .'

Keeping my glass of Coke back on the table, I told them the story of my first day in the kitchen, where I wanted to make a mixed-veg dish, but ended up preparing a hot pool of spicy, coloured water in which vegetables were swimming. Some of them were so over-boiled, they turned into paste and settled down at the bottom.

And, as was expected, everybody laughed at Day One of my Cookery Show. My Khushi, with a mouthful of soft-drink, was trying to, somehow, hold back her laughter. Pushkar laughed loudly and almost clapped his hands. It felt good.

And, soon, it was 2 p.m. No one realized how much time had passed—or, at least, I didn't.

'Lunch is ready,' Neeru announced.

By now I had made a little space in my tummy for the *rajma* which Khushi said she had made for me. She knew it was my favorite.

We all moved towards the dining table, pulled out the chairs and sat. And she sat right in front of me. I was looking at my future wife, thinking, 'A few months later, we will be having our lunch, dinner and breakfast together and, that too, in the same plate.'

Amused with the same thought, I opened the lid of the bowl in front me.

'Neeru, you also come,' said Ami di, taking some salad. The dining table was full of various dishes: *paneer, raita, aloo gobhi*, salad, a rice bowl along with a casserole of *chapattis* and my favorite *rajma*. The cutlery appeared new, the kind that was brought out for special occasions.

Everyone at the dining table was helping themselves and each other, passing the food stuff. I was trying to get a serving spoon from the other end of the table, when Khushi stopped me and silently said, 'Wait, I will get it.'

She picked up the spoon in one hand and a bowl in the other and served me. Then, she placed some salad on my plate, and asked me, '*Chapatti* or rice?'

I was looking at my caring sweetheart, who was helping me with my lunch. I was smiling inside, maybe even outside, and in my heart I asked her, 'You will always take care of me this way . . . Right?'

'*Chapatti* or Rice?' she again asked, raising her brows.

But who was hungry then? Her care and love for me had already filled me. Still, I said, 'A . . . A . . . *Chapatti*.'

With her beautiful hands she opened the casserole and quickly moved her hand back to avoid the hot steam. Her bangles tinkled. Then, with three fingers she folded two chapattis in half and, very gracefully, placed them on my plate. She looked at me and smiled. I wanted her to feed me with her own hands so that I could lick her beautiful fingers . . . All of a sudden, I wanted to marry her and marry her very soon. So that I could lie down in her lap. So that I could have my meals from her hands.

Everyone went ahead with the lunch. The moment I had that bite I knew those anxious eyes were expecting a response from me. I looked up into her charming eyes and told her I loved what she had prepared for me. She smiled and felt so satisfied when she noticed that I had the *rajma* before anything else. She then took her first bite, after I did.

We got busy with our meal and the conversation reduced and narrowed down to the appreciation of the lunch and the people who had prepared it. I believe it was quarter to three when we were through. I was all packed with delicious food, pudding and fruits (dessert, for which I struggled to make some space in my tummy).

Conversation resumed at the sofa and chairs again. This time it involved humor—good jokes, poor jokes, and jokes which were not jokes at all. Even her mother was laughing aloud, along with us youngsters. And, at times, I noticed a different smile. A smile which was not on her lips, but in her eyes. A smile which told me that she thought I was a nice guy. A smile which revealed that, soon, she would be prepared to give her daughter to me, for the rest of her life. A smile which was blessing me and her, for a bright future. And somewhere, silently, that smile also whispered in my ear the words from her heart, 'With her, I will be giving you my heart. Take care of her . . . Always'

It was 4 o'clock in the evening when we had a cup of tea. 'We', meaning Pushkar and I, as rest of them did not drink tea. Yes, no one in that entire family drinks tea. Strange family—that's what Pushkar and I feel.

Meanwhile, Khushi went to her room and, the very next moment, I was astonished to see her SMS on my cell. Wondering why she did that, I read the message.

I'll cal u in 2 min. u go out
in the veranda 2 receive d cal.
Don't let oders kno dat I m calin.

And she called me up.

I acted as if it was one of my college friends and, talking to this college friend of mine, I went out into the veranda, and from its furthest corner asked her, 'Where are you calling from?'

'Bathroom,' she replied.

'Wow! What are you doing there . . . ?' I asked mischievously.

'Shut up! Now listen to me,' she said, trying to explain something to me.

And, for the next minute, this is what I said:

'What!?'

'Are you crazy?'

'Wow!'

'But are you sure you will be able to do this?'

'Yes! Yes! I mean will WE be able to . . . ?'

'Oh Boy! I can't believe this. You have such guts. I would love to do this . . .'

'Thrilling! But what if we get caught?'

'Neeru? She will help us? Great! Your little sister rocks *yaar*.'

'All right, done. Let's do this in half an hour. You can call my cab right now.'

Thrilled and anxious because of her (I mean my college friend's) call, I returned to the drawing room. Everything was the same there—the environment, the talk and the people—but all of a sudden I wanted the time to pass quickly. I was excited about the plan (which also involved Neeru) that Khushi and I had just discussed. I kept wondering if we could really do it.

4.10 p.m.

To put our plan into action, we were waiting for Pushkar and Ami di's departure.

Every now and then, one of us would look at the wall clock or a wristwatch. That and a few quiet moments made them realize they were getting late. And . . .

Bingo!

Pushkar got up and said, looking at Ami di, 'I think we are getting late.'

Hearing that, Neeru looked at me with her twinkling eyes and I looked at Khushi. The three of us were ready for action.

4.12 p.m.

'Mumma! I have to leave for IMS,' Neeru said, like a kid who doesn't really want to do something.

'IMS?? Now? But you don't have classes in the evening *na*?' her mother asked.

'There is a doubt–clarification session today. Khushi also has a class. Ask her . . .'

'You also have to go?' Mumma asked Khushi.

'Class *to hai*, but I won't go if you don't want me to,' Khushi replied.

Meanwhile, I rushed in with my lines, 'No, no, I think you should go ahead with your class. Even I have to leave soon. A few minutes back, one of my college friends from Delhi called up and he wants to see me. I can't ignore him.'

Pushkar asked, 'How will you girls go then? Do you want me to drop you?'

Khushi replied immediately, 'No, Pushkar. You guys go ahead. IMS is in a totally opposite direction from where you are going. We will manage.'

4.15 p.m.

Things were going as per plan when Pushkar asked me, 'Ravin, how will you go back to Delhi?'

'Oh, I had called up a cab. I think it's there, outside,' I answered him, walking towards the door and looking out to confirm.

Looking at her sisters, Ami di said, 'Well, in that case, Ravin can drop you at IMS. It's on his way.'

And this was what we wanted to hear.

Ami di looked at me and I pretended that I didn't know. 'Oh! IMS will be falling on my way? In that case I can drop you,' I turned towards her sisters. It was getting hard to control our smiles, especially when everything was going as planned.

'You won't have any problem *na*?' Neeru asked.

And in my heart, I said, 'Come on! Don't overdo it, dumbo.' Aloud, I said, 'Oh come on! What problem can I have, in giving a lift to two gorgeous ladies? The pleasure will be mine.' I looked at everybody and smiled.

Khushi rushed to her room and came back in ten minutes, having changed. She looked stunning in her black top and white denim. She started moving from one room to another in search of her sandals. Still busy with her dressing up, she didn't notice me.

'*Chalo*, let me show you our room,' Neeru said and led me to her room, which she shared with Khushi. At the door, she gestured with her arm, 'This is our room,' making my eyes go from right to left.

While she talked about the different things present in her room, I was busy seeing something else. My eyes fell on the bed where there lay something so attention-grabbing, so fascinating. The pink and sky-blue suit, that my lady had taken off herself a few minutes back, was lying on her bed, inside out. It was spread upon the surface of the bed, covering half of it. I don't know why it was so exciting for me to gaze at the clothes which she had been wearing the entire day in front of me. Especially, turned inside turned out. Oh boy! The fact that, minutes before, she was in them and they were adhering to her body was sending waves of fantasy through me. A crazy, chilled and warm feeling, that they still were carrying her fragrance in them, in those wrinkles, in the threads of the stitches that were now visible, in that sweet wetness on the underarms. I wished I could touch them, feel them, breathe them. Had Neeru not been there, I would definitely not have been able to stop myself.

But I had to end my fantasy and look at what Neeru was showing me on her different shelves, her books, her computer and the rest of the room. I was still listening to Neeru when

Khushi came in, looking for us. She was now ready, with her sandals on.

The moment her eyes fell on the bed, she quickly rushed to grab her clothes.

'Shit!' she softly muttered, revealing her shyness at the favor she had unconsciously done for me. She then took them to the bathroom where she probably hung them behind the door. She thought I was busy talking to Neeru but, from the corner of my eyes, I noticed what she thought I didn't notice.

4.20 p.m.

By now we were at the door, almost done with our final goodbyes to everybody. Pushkar and Ami di got in their car. I touched Mumma's feet and she put her hands on my head. I said that I would see her after I came back from the US. She wished me a happy journey.

Khushi, Neeru and I then made a move towards my cab. The feeling of victory within us was at its peak then, when we found ourselves at the last step of our mission. Our immediate destination was the IMS center, where we would drop Neeru who would attend an unscheduled class in an unknown batch. And Khushi would not step out of the cab as she would be with me for the rest of the evening—without letting her family know. That was our plan.

But then, something happened the very moment we got into our cab and locked the doors—a contingency we hadn't even thought about, let alone planned for.

All of a sudden Khushi's mother remembered that she had to go to the dairy, from where she used to get milk, every evening, for their home. It would soon close down and, with no one left in the house, it would be a problem for her. And, unfortunately, I found out that, besides IMS, the dairy also fell on my route.

'Uh . . . ah . . . y . . . yes . . . we . . . We will drop her *na,*'
Khushi stammered, looking at Neeru and me, her eyes full of
questions to which neither of us had an answer.

The plan for her escape with me was now dangling on a
broken bridge, and we didn't have any idea what was going to
happen next. All we were wondering was: Could we get away
with it? How long would it take for the truth to come out?
Would we have to pile on more lies to conceal the first lie?
Then, Khushi whispered in my ear, making sure her mother
didn't notice, 'The dairy will come before IMS. Don't worry.'
We would be back on track after the dairy. Or so it seemed.

Khushi started explaining the route to the driver. At times, I
felt she was explaining more than necessary, talking too much.
I was not sure if it was her nervousness (her mother was with
us!) or her excitement (the plan could still work out!). Whatever
it was, it was making me a little conscious and I wished that
moment would soon pass. No sensible guy would want his
future mother-in-law to see him as a person who deceived her
and ran off with her daughter on the very first day.

But Khushi . . . I don't know what was wrong with her.
She was talking a lot. Talking to the driver, talking to Mumma,
talking to everyone. Talking, explaining. Explaining, talking.

And with so much explanation, the driver got little confused
and he ended up asking Neeru, who was sitting on the front seat,
'*Mataji to dairy tak jaayengi. Aur aap kahan tak jaaoge? Delhi tak?*'

And then the blunder happened.

My excited, talkative, nervous Khushi forgot, for a second,
the alibi we'd been building up for the last hour and said, before
Neeru had a chance to answer, '*Nahin bhaiyya, yeh to IMS pe
hi utar jaayegi.*'

Before she could understand what she had done, her mother
tapped her shoulder and asked, '*Ye to IMS pe hi utar jayegi
matlab? Tuney kahaan utarna hai fir?*' Of course her mother's

radar had become very active, trying to understand what was happening.

'*Gayi bhains paani mein,*' I heard Neeru say to herself without looking back. My expression said, 'Holy Shit!'

And Khushi.

Khushi bit her tongue, realizing the mess she had created. She took another name—a friend she was going to meet first, so that she could take her notes. But her mother had already smelled something fishy and she looked at Neeru and asked, 'Neeru. What's happening?'

And Neeru, helping her elder sister out of the mess, replied, 'Mumma, she has to get her maths notes from a friend, first.'

At that moment, the cab arrived at the dairy where their mother was to halt. I'm sure she wanted to say a lot of things to her daughters, especially the elder one but, because of my presence, she only said, 'Come back home on time. *Theek hai*?'

'*Haanji*. Yes, Mumma,' the females in the cab replied. And I bid goodbye to their mother for the last time.

A soon as she left and the cab moved on, Neeru and I both yelled, 'What the hell did you do!?'

Khushi looked down and said, 'Sorry,' like a kid whose parents have caught him breaking a window with his cricket ball.

'*Marte marte bache hain . . . Ye bhi naa,*' Neeru said.

Still, all of us were relieved by the narrow escape. But it was not an escape. Parents know their children so well. They have spent much more time than us in this world and, of course, if at our age we think we are smart, then at their age they are smarter. Her mother had understood very well that her elder daughter was definitely not heading towards IMS but someplace else. But that's the beauty of a mother's heart. She allowed her to go, without letting her know that she knew where her daughter was going.

Back in the cab, Neeru and I were laughing at Khushi's great work. I noticed the driver's smiling face in the rearview mirror. He had also figured out what we were up to. In another five minutes, we reached

IMS, where Neeru got down.

'Bye-bye beautiful,' I waved my hand.

'Byeeee,' she sang in her sweetest voice and reminded me, 'Bring me a ton of chocolates from the US.'

'I will, for sure,' I replied.

She then walked towards her destination and we moved towards ours—the hotel I was staying in, in Delhi. This part of the plan even Neeru didn't know about. All she was told by her sister was that we were going to watch a movie. A double-cross!

Khushi, again, touched my heart with this. I was happy seeing her excitement and satisfaction matching mine. My love had cooked up a story to spend time with her prince charming. (Oh, yes! I was given that title by my princess, that evening.) I appreciated her guts and her willingness to be with me. After all, she was the one who lied and planned things. The eagerness in her, to spend a few more moments with me, an evening . . . The trust she showed in me that day created an intangible bond between our hearts.

I turned towards her and saw that beautiful innocent face glowing with happiness. I was sitting by her side and it was like being in a beautiful dream. Yes, I know what was happening was all real. Yet, it was so magical. Even the air that surrounded us in the cab was different. I felt great and was glad that she was mine and I was with her. And, at that point of time, I never knew she was going to give me the best hour of my life.

At about 6 p.m. that evening, we reached my hotel. Before we got down, I asked the cabdriver to be back by 7.30 so that I could drop her home by 8.45 or so. According to the plan, her class at IMS was to last till 8.30 that evening.

Walking up the staircase of the hotel I felt a different feeling. I found myself among a different section of my friends. Friends who possessed a girlfriend, with whom they hung out in their cars, took them out to dinner, or maybe to a disco or a movie. Maybe their girlfriends had to lie to their families too, just like mine. I don't know why I never felt that way earlier. Khushi had been in my life for a couple of months by then. But I guess her presence in front of me was making me see myself in that class of my friends. And, to be honest, seeing myself in that category was exciting. With her in my life, the world appeared so good to me.

Walking together, we reached room 301 once again. I handed over the keys of the room to her—I wanted her to open my room.

We entered and I switched on the light. My room was a little messy, with many things dumped on the bed—the empty water bottle, a T-shirt, my cellphone's charger and hands-free set all tangled up with each other, the bed sheet half on the bed and half on the floor and some of my official, but not-so-important documents underneath my pillow.

'Sorry for this mess. I thought the hotel people would do this,' I said, rubbing my hand behind my neck.

She smiled, probably recalling how I used to boast that I was a neat and tidy guy. She could now see that with her own eyes.

'I'll be back in a minute,' I said and went to the washroom to wash my tired and oily face.

When I came out, two or three minutes later, I saw something which pleased me immensely. My room had been tidied up in those few minutes. From my bed, the things had returned to their proper places. The T-shirt in the closet, the charger wrapped and placed beside the TV on the TV set, the empty water-bottle in the dustbin, the official papers all piled up on the table beside the bed.

And who did that? Of course, it was the real neat and tidy person in that room.

Wow! Now that's what being with a girl is. I felt this for the very first time. This is what is called a woman's touch. This is why we keep hearing, 'Men build houses, but women make homes.' And now I had found one such woman.

A little later, we were sitting on the bed, with our feet in the channel between the two beds. On my laptop we were watching a dance video in which I had performed some time ago. It was a cultural festival back at Infosys. She was so excited to see me dancing and kept saying that if she happened to get on board at Infy, we will perform together at the next cultural meet. With those glittering eyes, she kept looking at the laptop's screen. And I kept looking at her . . .

I am still not sure what was so beautiful about the side of her neck, underneath her ear, to which her long earring was drawing my attention. I stared at her neck and I stared at it some more. Her beauty was trapping my senses. And my senses were freezing every second. She was still watching that video when I came very close to her neck and, without uttering a single thing, I kissed her there.

I did not see her expression then, as I was still feeling her neck and the sweet smell of her body. This happened in no time and she was not in a condition to react either. When she gained her senses in a while, she responded by raising her face, letting me get to her neck, beneath her chin, and I went ahead, kissing each and every cell of hers. Our eyes were closed. I grabbed her in my arms, felt her arms stiffening and gripping tightly the corner of my shirt, her voice expressing what she felt.

The video on my laptop was still running, but it failed to interrupt us.

She almost left herself in my hands. I leaned on her a bit and she leaned on the bed, our feet still touching the ground. She crossed her hands around my neck and my hands were supporting her body. Together we were sliding down, every single second. The kisses and passionate hugs continued till we fell on the bed.

Suddenly, I remembered something. 'I'll come in a second, just a single second,' I whispered in her ear. Her eyes were still closed. And I went and checked and double-locked the room. I switched off our room's bright light and switched on the washroom's light allowing it to illuminate our room softly. I did that for a reason which I did not tell her—memories from a movie were bothering me, in which a hidden camera in a hotel room captured a couple.

Then I came back to her. But her eyes were not closed any more. She was staring at me as I walked towards her. Holding her hands in mine I stood by her and looked into the depth of her eyes. And, for the first time, I noticed something different in them. I saw a girl in whose heart fear had entered. Then I realized what caused it. The innocent girl, whom I saw in those eyes, was afraid of being with a guy, especially on his bed, in a closed room, double-locked, which was not even lit properly, but illuminated by a dim light seeping in from the washroom's open door. She did not say anything, but I saw everything that was going through her mind at that instant.

'Shona . . .' she said, and I gently whispered 'Ssshhh!' and placed my hand upon her lips, not allowing her to speak. I ran my palm across her forehead and very gently closed her eyes once more, my fingers flowing on her eyelashes. Then I said to her, very softly, 'You know what? I won't do anything which our conscience and values don't allow. I just can't. For the simple reason that I love you. I know my limits and I promise nothing will happen to make you feel uncomfortable, nothing that you will regret later. I promise . . . Just be with me in this moment.' And my angel wrapped me in her arms, pulling me closer to her.

'Shona!' she called my name with such affection. 'I love you so very much, for everything you do for me.' I felt her hands crawling on my back. Her fear had disappeared and she was celebrating having me in her arms.

I was lying partly on the bed and partly on her. She was becoming mischievous and I was no different. Neither of us knew when the video in my laptop stopped. But the moment I realized this, without her noticing, I ran my favorite soundtrack's playlist on my laptop at a low volume, adding to the romantic ambience of the room.

Everything was just perfect—a dimly lit room, light music running in the background, nice bed sheets, and she and I.

I blew upon her eyes, which made her lashes go down further, gently closing her eyes. That wisp of air moved on her forehead from left to right, back to her eyes, then her cute nose, making an irregular figure on her cheeks, scrolling between her lips and riding her chin from where it slid down to her neck and was lost in the air between us. She opened her eyes again. I touched her nose with mine after which I rubbed it against hers, just like mothers do to their beautiful babies to express their love. She, too, was a beautiful baby. My baby. She smiled with that mischievous shyness.

What a beautiful moment that was! And, of course, I had to make it a memorable one, and how could that be without a kiss? And that's why, in no time, I thought of so many things to make it a perfect kiss . . . I'll do this . . . I'll do that . . . I will embrace her this way, hold her face that way . . . and then . . . So much planning for a kiss. And, then, I went for it.

Soon, our faces were close to each other, slightly tilted at opposite angles, our warm breaths falling on each other's lips. My lips touched hers. I kissed her. And I kissed her again.

I don't remember when I closed my eyes and I was lost in her. That moment was a heaven that I knew for the first time in my life. In that moment, I forgot everything, forgot everything that I had planned a few minutes back. Forgot even the fact that I had planned something. Forgot that the next day I was to leave this country. Forgot my job, the CAT exam, forgot my friends and my family. Forgetting everything, I lived that one moment . . . The best hour of my life.

I don't remember whether I opened my eyes first, or she did. But we were looking into each other's eyes.

I was still lying on her.

She smiled, I smiled.

She blinked her eyes, I blinked mine.

Kissing my forehead one more time, she said, 'I love you soooooooooo much, Shona.'

And I rubbed my nose against hers one more time and repeated, 'I love you so so so so much, sweetheart.'

We had been so busy with our romance that we forgot to look at the time. We had asked the cab driver to be there at the hotel entrance by

7.30. The wall clock in front of me said it was 8.30. 'Uh-oh! Do you know what time it is?' I asked, very casually, smiling. She immediately looked at the clock. And then she screamed, just like the way she did the day before.

'EIGHT THIRTY????'

And with that, she got up from the bed, panicked, rushed here and there grabbing her belongings, her cell, her purse, her sandals . . . and a lot more. I switched on the lights to help her.

She then rushed to the washroom, splashed a little water on her face, used the spare towel hanging behind the door, pulled a comb out of her purse, got her hair done, pulled out a lipstick and daubed it on her lips.

Watching her, I wondered how much lipstick I had swallowed and I laughed at myself without saying anything. As she was getting ready, I picked up her purse. 'Boy! Seems like a magical purse. So many things are coming out of it—comb, lipstick, hanky . . . Let me see what else is left in this,' I said laughing.

And at that very moment, she slapped my hand which was trying to unzip the purse. 'Bad manners! A boy should never check a girl's purse.' 'But, why? Do you girls carry bombs in your purses?' I said handing it over. 'Even at my office, they have appointed a lady at the gate to check the purses of all the girls. I wonder what funny things those girls show her in their purses . . . they smile looking at her and then she smiles back at them.' I laughed at my joke, but she didn't.

She was worried about getting late. I noticed that and, parking my lavish laughter somewhere, tried to console her with a smile, 'It's ok, Khushi. Relax. We'll reach your place before 10 p.m. Don't worry, dear.'

Wearing her sandals, she said, 'Shona, if we don't reach on time and they find out at home, *na*, I'll be in big trouble.'

Seeing her in this state I went close to her and put my hands on her shoulders. 'Khushi. Everything is going to be fine. No matter what, you won't be in any trouble. I promise. Will you trust me now?' I gently asked her.

And very innocently she nodded her head.

'Take a deep breath, have a sip of water and we will move out.'

A few minutes later we were in the back-seat of our cab.

'*Bhaiyya*, back to Faridabad, from where we came,' Khushi said to the driver, in haste.

But, as we found out when we came out of the hotel, it had rained heavily during the past hour. Water was flushing down from the corners of the roofs of nearby buildings, rattling down pipes from various floors to the common ground. Manholes on the roads were open to let the accumulated water on the streets drain out.

Our cab started rolling.

'*Bhaiyya,* how long will it take?' she asked the driver.

'*Kuch keh nahin sakte, madam. Bahut baarish hui hai. Bus aagey road pe kahin jam na laga ho.*'

The thought of a possible traffic jam worried her all the more. She looked at me. And I told her to relax. 'I am there with you, right? So why are you worried? We'll reach on time.'

Hearing my tone, the driver too realized that he should not scare her. In fact, he added, '*Madam, ghabraane waali to koi baat hi nahin hai. Hum pahunch jaayenge.*'

But soon we found ourselves in trouble. About fifteen minutes from my hotel we got stuck in a traffic jam—probably the biggest I have ever seen in my life. There were hundreds of cars in front of us, I'm sure. A horrible jam. Water rushed over the roads towards the drains. Everything out there was wet. The shops were closing; their wet shutters were rolling down. The cars, big and small, struggled to find their way. None of the vehicles on that road stayed in line. Everyone was on their own, finding a little space for themselves, competing with each other because of which no one was able to move ahead. What a mess!

'A truck's engine has failed to start, half a kilometer ahead,' we heard, when our driver rolled his window down. Hearing this, almost everyone switched off their engines. Inside our cab, the mercury of panic and helplessness was rising.

Half an hour after the most wonderful time together in my hotel room, we were now entering a phase full of anxiety and despair. With me was a girl who had lied to her family and managed to escape with me. Apart from her office, she had never stayed out so late at any other place. But that day, she was in another state and the guy she had put all her trust in (of course, me) was not familiar with the city. And time . . . Time was running fast in my wrist watch, but stood stagnant when I glanced at the traffic around us. Fifteen minutes passed and our cab did not move an inch. It would be wrong to say that I was not panicking. But I was aware of my responsibilities. I was responsible for Khushi's safety.

Eventually, our cab driver also switched off the cab's engine which raised the already high levels of anxiety within us still higher. Somehow, a running engine in a traffic jam still appears more hopeful than a switched-off one. Of course, it's all psychological but, unfortunately, it made an impact on both of us.

And since it never just rains, but it pours—Khushi's cellphone started ringing.

She looked at me in fear. I looked at my watch. It was close to 9 p.m.

'What if it's Mumma's phone?' she asked, worried and all I could say was, 'First see who's calling.'

She opened her purse and breathed a sigh of relief. 'Thank God! It's Neeru.'

She put the phone on speaker. Clearing her throat and recovering her strength (which she lost when she heard the ring), she said, 'Neeru.'

'Where are you, *yaar*?' Neeru asked.

'*Yaar*, we're stuck in a traffic jam.'

'But you're in Faridabad only *na*?'

'*Haan baba* . . . We went to see a movie. Meanwhile it rained heavily and all the water on the road has caused a traffic jam and we're stuck.'

'*Theek hai*, but come home quickly. I have reached home and have told Mumma that your doubt class got delayed and you'll reach here in another twenty–thirty minutes.'

'Thanks. We're just waiting for this jam to clear. I'll be home soon,' Khushi said and hung up.

Twenty–thirty minutes!? Nobody could drive to Faridabad that fast, even if the roads were completely empty. Even Khushi knew that.

'Shona, I'm feeling very tense,' she said, her voice scared and soft.

But obviously we'd be tense. Still, I said, 'I know dear. But we should not lose patience. In the worst case, we'll reach your place a little late, right? Don't worry. If that happens, I will explain everything to Mumma. *Theek hai*?' I tried to console her, raising my hand to move her head close to me so that she could rest on my shoulder.

The next moment we noticed the traffic moving ahead from one corner of the road. Like everyone else, our driver started the engine and followed the herd of the vehicles. A ray of hope brightened our faces.

In a while our driver gave us a reason to bolster our smile. '*Sahib ab nikal jaayenge aaraam se, jam khul gaya hai. Bas ek baar border cross kar lein. Phir highway theek hai.*'

He was referring to the Delhi–Haryana border which we successfully crossed in another 20 minutes. But our destination was still miles away.

Her head was still on my shoulder and I kept talking to her, trying to divert her mind. She was moving her fingers on my palm, drawing imaginary lines, playing like a kid. When she reached my third finger, she started playing with the ring I was wearing. It was an unusual ring with three intersecting silver circles, just like the Olympic circles.

When she asked me about that ring, I took it as an opportunity to divert her from the panic of the moment and started telling her a little story about my ring which became as mysterious as *The Lord of the Rings*.

'Aaah!' I said, as if she had stepped on a broken limb.

'What happened?' she asked, raising her head from my shoulder.

'Nothing,' I replied very sadly, turning my head to the other side, looking outside the cab's window.

Surprised by my reaction, she did not say anything but waited for me to speak. And I did, saying, 'I knew, someday I would have to tell you about this . . .'

This statement raised her eyebrows and she insisted I tell her everything. I kept looking out of the window and she kept asking me to reveal the story behind it. '*Bataao na* Shona . . . Tell me please . . .'

I was killing time. The cab was speeding ahead. And thoughts were running through her mind about the mystery ring on my third finger. More so, because I appeared so reluctant to tell her.

'Shona tell me *na* . . . *kya baat hai*,' she again asked, turning my face towards her with her hand.

'Khushi . . .' I said, looking at her.

'Hmm . . . ?'

'Almost a year back, before I met you . . . Before I met you . . . I mean . . . It was like . . . One day a beautiful girl put this ring on my finger . . .' and I turned away, avoiding her eyes and looking outside the cab again.

Silence . . .

She was still listening—all ears—forgetting completely that we were getting late.

Looking out of the cab I continued, 'I always wanted to tell you this, but . . . but never got a chance, for I didn't know how you will feel about all this.'

Her eyes were staring at me with so many questions.

The next second, her cellphone rang. It was Neeru again, saying how their mom was getting restless and the fact that, by now, she knew well enough that Khushi had not been to IMS but somewhere else with me. She also said that it was raining heavily in Faridabad. And all that Khushi told her was to manage the situation somehow, 'Tell her that I am stuck in the rain.' Sweet Neeru was bouncing like a shuttle between her mother and her sister. This is the fate of being the youngest in the family—everyone tends to push you around.

The moment she hung up, she returned to the earlier topic.

'A girl gave you this?' she asked, looking at the ring and then at me. That wasn't her only question, though. There was a fusillade, ready for me. And I kept beating around the bush. This went on for some 15 minutes, when she finally asked me, pulling my hand over her head, 'Swear on me, did a girl slip this on your finger?'

So much expectation in her eyes. Expectation that I should speak the truth. And also the expectation that my answer should be a big 'No'—which would have meant that my entire story was a lie meant only to scare her. But, breaking her second expectation, I nodded my head, acknowledging that all she heard was true.

Pin-drop silence . . .

The environment inside the cab now was much more tense. The traffic jams, reaching home late, standing before her mother to admit her lie, all of this appeared so minuscule in front of this giant truth. The girl, who was in my arms so passionately an hour ago, was now facing such a different truth. I expected her to shout at me, to yell at me, to do something before I told her. And I wanted this to continue for a few more miles.

And I was doing that for a reason. The more time I consumed, the lesser she would have worried about reaching home so late. It was already 10 p.m.

But when that sweet and innocent heart sobbed, when the first tear came out of those beautiful eyes, I had to break the mystery. How could I see her crying?

'Hey Shonimoni . . . Listen to me.' And I took her in my arms and said, 'All that you heard was true, but in a totally different aspect. You have to know the complete story.'

'Tell me then,' she said, rubbing her eyelash like a kid, her eyes on me again.

'The girl who slipped this on . . . I don't even know her name. I hardly met her for ten minutes. Almost a year back, I was at Waterloo station in London along with my friend, waiting for my train to Belgium. Because my train was a little late, my friend and I visited a little stall on the platform near us. A girl in that stall was selling rings. From the display, I liked this one and picked it up. But I was wondering how to wear this ring with three circles. To help me, she held my hand and slipped it on. It looked good. I thanked her, paid her five pounds and walked away to catch my train.'

With that, my tense expression turned into a mischievous one and I noticed the curve of her lips expanding every microsecond. Her wet eyes were now glittering again.

'One more thing . . .' I interrupted her smile. 'That girl . . . She was damn beautiful!' And I laughed.

And she laughed too, punching me on my chest and shoulders. 'Youuuu . . . You know how badly you scared me? I'm gonna kill you,' she kept shouting at me and punching me while I was trying to safeguard myself.

But the next minute, her cell rang again and on its screen was flashing 'Neeru calling . . .'

Khushi took the call and said, 'Neeru . . . I'm just about to reach . . . And listen . . .'

She did not complete her line but paused then and there. It wasn't Neeru, but her mom.

The fear returned to her face. She was shaking. Patting the shoulder of the driver she gestured him to mute the radio, and with a finger on her lips told me to stay silent. Then she put her cell on speaker again. It was 10.10.

She tried hard to convince her mom that she was still at IMS, stuck in the rain. I don't know how successful she was. It was getting difficult for her to hide the truth. The last thing she told her mom was not to worry as her entire batch was with her, after which both of them hung up.

All my effort to divert her attention to something else with my ring story crashed in a minute. While she kept her cell back in her purse, the driver turned the radio on again, at a low volume.

By then we were on Mathura Road, heading towards her home in Faridabad.

'*Bhaiyya*, how much more time?' she asked the driver.

But the driver did not respond and I sensed something was very wrong.

A never-ending pool of water was in front of us, covering everything on the ground. The road had disappeared and even the divider was submerged. Our cab was, even now, running on water-covered road. Every single minute, the water level was increasing, reaching almost a foot. The culprit was Faridabad's fabulous drainage system.

There were no street lights on that road. Or if there were, they were out of order. In that pool of water, there were various vehicles struggling to move ahead, inch by inch. In the headlights of our cab I saw waves in the water, carrying leaves and stems of small creepers and weeds, beating against the bodies of the vehicles stuck in the spate. The cab was still going ahead, at a slower speed. We were moving into deeper water now and, finally, the driver said he couldn't go ahead. '*Sahib ye choti gaadi hai, engine mein paani chala jaayega. Hum aur aagey nahin jaa sakte.*'

I tried to persuade him to go ahead but he was adamant and I got furious. '*Bhaiyya. Is vakt na, mera dimaag bahot jaada kharaab ho raha hai, aur agar fir se tumne ye kaha naa . . .*' I said to him, losing my patience, when Khushi held my wrist stopping me from saying any more. She knew we did not have any option but to survive on the driver's mood. So I changed my tone and told him in a gentlemanly way, '*Bhaiyya, mujhe sirf inhe ghar tak pahonchaana hai. Aap please aagey chalte raho. Agar aapki cab kharaab hui to jo bhi kharcha hoga vo main de dunga.*'

With my pleading, somehow he agreed to move ahead. He drove the cab further but the going was very slow.

It was 10.30 now. I knew that our situation was tense, and I was sick and tired of being tense.

Our cab was stuck in that messy pool when, all of a sudden, a truck passed us on our left. I saw those giant wheels churning the water like a turbine, generating big waves of water. I was trying to show Khushi those circular waves, whose circumference was exponentially rising from my left to her right, when I felt my socks getting wet inside my shoes.

'What the fuck!?'

The dirty water on the road was now seeping into our cab. Water, water and more water . . . Everywhere. Bubbling sounds came from under the cab's doors. Our feet were dipped in water, like tea bags in a cup of tea.

'Shit . . . so much water?' she screamed.

We took off our shoes and lifted our legs up on the seats.

'*Yeh to hona hi tha,*' the driver said.

At that time, we were not very far from her house. On a normal day, it would have been a fifteen-minute drive. But stuck in that disaster, it was hard to predict how long it would take.

Gradually, the view outside our cab was getting even worse. One by one, almost all of the vehicles stopped moving. Their engines took their last breaths and failed to start again. I saw people getting out of their cars and pushing them from behind, in order to get them out of that pool. It was a complete mess. People, with their trousers rolled up to their knees, barefoot, out of their vehicles, were shouting at each other for various

reasons and for no reason. Some of them had even taken off
their shirts.

The few, who were still behind the steering wheel, were
struggling hard to drive and constantly cursing each other,
especially the autorickshaw-*wallas*. '*Tere baap ki sadak hai*?' '*Abey
saaley peeche hatt*!' '*Arey teri maa ki . . .*' They were getting into
fights, leaving behind their dead autos.

Back in the cab our minds were tense and tired of the events
of the last two hours. Looking at her then, I found her hands
joined and eyes closed. She was praying to God. She was very
scared. And maybe her prayers were being heard. Maybe that
was why our small cab was still moving ahead in the water when
almost all the small cars on that road had broken down.

Meanwhile, she got another call from her mother, who was
now more furious and more worried. And when she said that
she had called up Khushi's cousin (who also lived in Faridabad)
to go to IMS and bring her home, we had to reveal the truth.

Taking a deep breath Khushi said, '*Mumma, main IMS mein
nahin hun. Main Ravin ke saath hun . . . shaam se. I am sorry ki
maine aapko jhoot bola.*'

I held her hand in my hand. We were both scared of what
her mother's reaction would be.

And Khushi told me, after the call, that, surprisingly, her
mother relaxed when she heard the truth. Maybe she thought
that her daughter was with someone she thought she could trust.
The city was not safe for women, especially at night, when the
savages of the city came out of their dens and did all manner
of ill. So, maybe, her mother felt some comfort knowing I was
with Khushi.

But the 'truth' we told her on the phone was still a half-truth.

When asked where we had been till then, Khushi told her
what she told Neeru, 'Mumma . . . we went to watch a movie.

And when we came out, it had rained so much, there was water everywhere, and then the traffic jam . . .'

While she was convincing her mom, she stole a moment to whisper in my ears, 'We had been to see *Munnabhai*, all right?'

And I loved her for this very reason. The way she had the guts to take all sorts of risks to make me feel happy, to make me enjoy that day of my life with her, and to endure scoldings from her family for that . . . I felt blessed to have her in my life.

Once that confession-call ended, we felt relaxed, as if we had got a weight off our hearts.

We had just taken a left turn to enter her street when our cab suddenly tilted to the left. The three of us slid down towards our left and our hands grabbed our seats, trying to keep our bodies upright. More water rushed in. There was now about half a foot of water in the cab. Our shoes were floating somewhere inside.

Our tilted cab failed to move ahead, no matter how much the driver accelerated. The left front-wheel seemed to be stuck in a pothole. In order to move ahead, the driver asked me to push the cab from behind. So I jumped out into the puddle. It felt just like jumping into the shallow end of a swimming pool except, in a swimming pool, the water is not so dirty and you are not in your jeans and shirt.

I stood barefoot in that puddle. My feet touched small stones with sharp edges and some bushy stuff which might have been weeds or some small, watery insects. It was a little scary. The water came up to my thighs. Even rolling up the jeans to my knees did not serve any purpose. I went behind the cab. The driver was still accelerating hard and Khushi kept saying, '*Shona . . . Sambhaal ke . . . Dhyaan se.*'

I pushed the cab hard, but nothing happened.

'*Sahib aur jor se . . .*' shouted the driver from inside.

Of course, he was shouting and talking to me. But I was lost in my thoughts . . .

I was supposed to catch my flight in six hours. I should have been back in my hotel room in Delhi, taking a nap so that I could wake up by 4 a.m. and go to the airport. But I was far away, stuck on a road in a different city, in wet jeans, a wet shirt and, perhaps, wet innerwear too, standing in a never-ending dirty pond, pushing a cab to take my girlfriend back to her home.

To be honest, I had no hopes of making it to the airport in the morning. Of course the trip to the States was important and, for that, catching the flight a few hours from now was important, and for that returning to the hotel in Delhi was important but, above all, to get her home was the most important.

'*Sahib aur jor se . . .*' shouted the driver one more time.

Finally, we were successful in getting the cab out. I observed Khushi, who had turned around in her seat and was looking at me, breathing a sigh of relief.

The depth of water on the street ahead was terrifying. Going on in that small cab did not look like a good decision at all. After a little brainstorming we concluded that rest of the distance could only be crossed by rickshaw. Because of its big wheels a rickshaw seemed to be the only viable option. So I walked down the road, still barefoot, to find a rickshaw. And I happened to find one, with much difficulty, but the rickshaw-*walla* did not agree to drive on that flooded street. When he finally did agree, it was because I paid him ten times the normal fare and, that too, in advance. My necessity was his opportunity.

I sat on the rickshaw and got back to the cab. I noticed blood on my right foot—I had a cut on my right toe. But there were other things to worry about. Back at the cab, I asked the driver to wait for me till I came back after dropping her home. I took his cell number and gave him mine.

Khushi got out of the cab and sat on the rickshaw. She was so shocked by everything that was happening that she forgot to get her sandals and it took me a few minutes to find them. (Searching for your girlfriend's footwear in the back of a car, your hands dipped in a dirty pool of water . . . Who says love is always a pleasant experience!)

The water level on this street was the highest and I warned the rickshaw-walla, '*Bhaiya yahaan par jaraa dhyaan se . . .*' The wheels of the rickshaw were almost submerged in the water and, at times, the water was splashing at our feet. The rickshaw puller's thighs moved in and out of the water on the road as he paddled strenuously. But we were making progress and, in another five minutes, our journey was going to end.

And with that would end our being together, so close to each other for so long that day. In the next few minutes I was going to see her for the last time, before I left the country. All this was running through our minds.

And that instant turned into an emotional, romantic moment.

Other than our rickshaw, there was no vehicle in that deserted street filled with water. Submerged, the entire street appeared so desolate. A different kind of silence prevailed and the loudest noise was the churning of the water from the wheels of our rickshaw. The moon in the sky above saw us together, in that hard time, attempting to get out of it, our care for each other. She was resting her head on my shoulder, her hands were in my lap. With my right arm around her shoulder I was supporting her as the rickshaw made its way on the uneven road. And in my other hand I was holding her sandals.

Taking her sandals from my hand and dropping them on the footrest of the rickshaw, she held my hand and said, 'Shona! Our love story is so different . . . Isn't it?'

'Hmm . . .' I smiled.

'The way we found each other,' she said.

'The way we kept talking on the phone and chatting for the past few months,' I added.

'The coincidences.'

'The way we fell in love without even seeing each other.'

'The way we finally met and spent the entire day.'

'And the way we are now.'

Indeed, everything was so different about our love story.

'Can I say something, Khushi?'

'Yes,' she said with such warmth.

'I am glad that such a night came in our life. You know why? After our marriage, sitting together on our terrace on beautiful nights, we will recall this hard time so many times . . . I feel so good that I am able to get you back to your place,' I said.

She pulled my hand towards her and kissed it.

'Now, can I say something?' she asked me.

'Hmm . . . Yes.'

'I am so fortunate to have you in my life. The way you take care of me, protect me, love me . . . I know our relationship does not need words like 'thank you' and 'sorry' but there is one thing which you did today and won my heart, for which I can't help thanking you.' She paused for a while and then said, 'Shall I tell you what it was?'

'Hmm.'

'I really wanted to thank you for those beautiful words you whispered in my ear, in your room. That you wouldn't do anything our conscience did not permit. You won my heart one more time when you promised me that there would be nothing that I did not like, nothing that I'd regret later. For a girl, those words mean a lot and I am glad you said them. I love you so much but, more than that, I respect you for what you are.'

She opened her heart to me. In that moonlight, sitting beside her on that rickshaw, sailing in that pool of water, I realized how happy she was. Maybe that's why her eyes got wet and happiness dropped off her eyelashes.

'I love you Shona . . . Always be with me in good times and in bad, just the way you are now,' she said.

'I promise,' I said, wiping her tears.

Our romantic, moonlight safari ended when we reached her home. At the gate were Neeru and her mother who, after breathing a sigh of relief on seeing her daughter, walked back inside showing her motherly anger.

We got down and I asked the rickshaw-*walla* to wait for five minutes.

At the gate I asked Neeru, 'What's her mood?'

'Till now she was worried, but now it's time for her to show anger. But she won't say much because you're here,' Neeru replied, smiling.

'*Chal*, I'll take care of that. But hey! Thank you sooooooooo much for helping us so far.'

And the three of us marched in, with me in front.

I saw Mumma sitting in the drawing room. Without caring that my wet jeans were spoiling their carpet, I went to her. Just like any mother in this world would have felt, she too was angry. Without saying a word to her, I kneeled down in front of her. Yes, I was on my knees in front of my future mother-in-law, looking in her eyes.

Very politely I told her, '*Khushi ki koi galti nahi hai is mein. Ye saara plan mera tha.* And you can punish me for that.' (And I said to myself, 'Please do it fast, I have to catch my plane in a few hours.')

Standing at the door, both the sisters looked at me. I don't know what they thought. Was I brave or stupid? I did not want Khushi to keep answering her mother's questions after my departure so I tried to sort things out, as far as possible, while I was present. I did what I felt would safeguard her.

The next moment, Mumma helped me get up and said, '*Ise itna pyaar karti hu naa, isliye itni chinta hoti hai iski. Thodey dino mein chale jaana hai isne yahaa se aapke ghar . . .*' She melted inside, thinking about her beloved daughter. All mothers are so emotional, even mine was.

She further said that we could have told her the truth and then left in the evening. She wouldn't have said no. ('Of course, she would not have said no for *Munnabhai*, but what about Delhi?' I was still talking to myself.)

Well, that's how I handled the situation back at her place. When I checked my watch next, it was midnight and I had to leave for Delhi, crossing the same pool of water, the same brawls and the same border, in the same watery car. Time was still running out and, if everything went well, I would be at Indira Gandhi International Airport in another five hours.

The atmosphere at her place was much better now. I walked down to the bathroom, badly needing to pee. Of course, being in those wet jeans for almost two hours and surrounded by water and more water, it was only natural.

A little later, back at the main gate, all the three ladies waved me goodbye. But I waved to the one standing ahead of everybody. I felt so different again. I was waving to the girl with whom I spent the longest day of my life, the girl with whom I enjoyed the best hour of my life. And I kept looking at her till my rickshaw took a left turn and she slipped out of my field of vision and I from hers.

In a short while, I was back in the cab. The water level on road had gone down and the conditions were better now. We didn't have too many problems going back. The traffic was negligible by then, though I still saw a few dead vehicles on either side of the road.

Every fifteen–twenty minutes, Khushi kept calling me on my mobile to check if everything was fine. She told me she was out of her wet attire and was lying in her cute night dress on her cosy bed. I loved it when she said that. It felt like being with her again. We couldn't talk too long though, as my cellphone's battery was dying.

I asked the driver to switch on the radio, wanting to celebrate the victory of the day or, probably, one of the memorable victories of my life. Sitting beside the driver I pulled back my seat to stretch my aching, wet legs. Tapping my feet (and the injured toe) gently to the music. I looked in the rearview mirror, on my left and I saw a reflection . . .

A reflection of the lights, of those vehicles struggling in the water, a reflection of the moment when she was resting her head on my shoulder in the rickshaw, a reflection of the time I was pushing the cab, of the calls from her home which we were too scared to pick up. A reflection of that perfect kiss in Room No. 301, that evening.

And, watching those reflections, I smiled and closed my eyes.

'Oh! Mumma . . . She is so perfect!'

I was at the airport, the last person in the long queue heading towards the British Airways terminal. I was struggling with the laptop hanging on my shoulder, pushing the trolley with the same hand and talking to my mom and dad on my cell. Outside, it was still dawn. The sun would rise in a few minutes. And I was damn sleepy. But the cold shower in the hotel helped me wake up. And to push me into the shower was Khushi, who woke me up at 4 a.m. sharp.

Back in my hometown, mom and dad were anxious to know what happened. Dad seemed to be enjoying my anecdotes much better than his morning news, otherwise he'd never ask mom to put my call on the speaker while he had his morning tea. How is her family? How is her Mumma? What did everyone say? What is their house like? And the craziest question was my mom's: What did you have for lunch there?

(God! Lunch?)

'Her family is really nice. I met her mother, her elder sister Ami di and Ami di's husband Pushkar. Her younger sister Neeru was also there. Her mom is just like you. I liked each one of them. Khushi is a very nice girl, Mumma . . . And I am very happy,' I said after which Mumma said, 'If you are happy, we are happy.'

And the happier they were, the more they questioned me. It took me almost half an hour to answer all their queries before I bade them goodbye and they wished me a happy journey.

After a little while, I felt like calling her. Though I knew she would be sleeping. While I slept in peace for three hours in my hotel room, she was checking her cell's clock every now and then so that she could wake me up on time. Now it was her turn to sleep in peace. Still, I dialed her number. Because in another couple of hours, I wouldn't be able to call her up.

I heard her complete ring, but did not get to hear her voice.

Disappointed, I slipped my phone back in my pocket and moved ahead. People were shoving their trolleys with one hand, their passport and tickets in the other. Some were enjoying the music flowing out of their iPods. Indian faces, non-Indian faces. The white kids stood silently in the queue, holding their parents' hands. The rest of the little ones running here and there, shouting, playing, were all Indian.

I was at the X-ray scanner, waiting for my baggage to slide out, when I heard my cell ringing. It was her.

'*Uth gaya mela baby . . .* ?'

'Hmm . . .' And in her warm, sleepy, heavy voice she was kissing me, probably with her eyes half-open, still tired. Hearing the sweetness of her voice, I imagined waking up next to her, on the same bed, some morning.

Clearing her throat, she then started talking to me.

My queue kept moving and we kept talking.

At the baggage check-in section, she was still with me.

At the immigration desk, she was still with me.

At the security check gateway, the officials separated her from me. They asked me to switch off the cellphone before the check. But the moment I was through with it, she was with me again. I badly wanted to talk to her, I badly needed her and I wanted to run away from the airport straight back to her. Actually, I felt like marrying her then and there. I was so much with her for those one and half hours that I didn't even notice the third and final announcement, meant for me. The last words were:

'. . . Boarding Flight No. BA182 to New York, please report at gate no. 2.'

I know my next statement will be hard to believe, but this is true. Miles away from me, lying on her bed in a different city, she heard my name being announced (which I had missed, though the speaker box was right above me), through my cellphone. Unbelievable, isn't it?

'Shona, I think it's for you,' she panicked.

'What?'

'That announcement. I think it's for you,' she shouted in haste.

'Just a second.'

I patted the back of a white-skinned man in front of me. He had a US flag on his T-shirt. '*Wudgyaa mind tellin me whom they were caallin for?*' I don't know why but talking to *goras* tends to change my accent.

'Oh, you mean the last call?'

'Yeah.'

'Some Ravin to New York. For fuck's sake, why are people not on time at the airport?'

And I kept looking into his eyes with anger but didn't say anything. Of course, the fault was mine.

'That's me,' I said firmly, getting closer to his face. 'But you know, hey . . . Thanks for letting me know that it was me.'

His face was something to be seen. Pale. Maybe, for a second, he remembered that he wasn't on his land but mine. But before he could start apologizing, I rushed to gate no. 2.

On the call, Khushi was still waiting for my response.

But, what happened next at the gate was surprising.

'Khushi, I'll call you back in a while,' I said and disconnected the call still trying to understand what happened.

The security lady at the door had taken my boarding pass, swiped it through a gadget which punched a single word, in bold red letters, on it. INVALID. She then returned it to me with a smile on her face. I looked at the pass and then at her face and wondered—Now what the hell was this? Then, she snatched it back from me and tore it into two pieces, stylishly, and dropped them into the dustbin beside her desk.

I was completely puzzled. Did they find some drugs in my baggage? Or some smuggled diamonds? Or may be a hand-grenade? Jesus! I don't even know what grenades look like.

Seeing the restlessness on my face the lady finally revealed what was going on.

'Congratulations, sir! You are our lucky passenger. You won't be traveling in Economy, but in the Business class.'

With a smile, she handed me a Business class boarding-pass and asked me to move ahead to the plane. The rest of the population, the poor economy class one's who were made to wait just because of me, were then allowed to follow.

What a surprise!

Moments later, I was in the plane and Khushi was with me again. I told her about my good luck and she promptly said, 'Because I'm in your life, only good things will happen to you.'

While talking to her I saw the same passenger passing by—the one with the US flag on his T-shirt. I waved to him sarcastically and he moved ahead to economy class as if he hadn't seen me. But I knew he had.

Thirty minutes later, the plane was good to take off. By then, one of the air-hostesses had already told me, twice, to switch off my mobile. But I was like, 'Who cares?' I was still busy with my romance on the phone.

When the plane was on the runway, the air hostess pleaded with me again to switch off my cell. I am sure she must have wondered who allowed me into the Business Class. I was behaving like a school kid whom teachers tend to compare to a dog's tail—no matter how you try, it can never be straight.

This time, though, I gestured her to come closer and asked her, 'Have you ever fallen in love?' I whispered in her ears.

'What?' She took a step back.

'On the other end is my girlfriend, whom I will marry some day. I won't be seeing her for a long time and these are the few, final moments before I leave this country. And in these moments she wants to be with me. Shall I tell her that a beautiful air hostess is commanding me not to talk to her?'

She smiled at me and went away. And in a few seconds she returned with a tall glass of juice and some cookies. Helping me with the blanket, especially covering my mobile and the hands-free wires, she whispered, 'Enjoy your moments with these.'

And of course I enjoyed my moments with Khushi. She kept kissing me and I was bidding her goodbye before the network got disconnected.

The plane took off.

Away from Her

Day One

I remember well. It was Saturday evening, around 7.30 p.m., when I checked into my hotel. At the reception, while making the payment with a few travelers' cheques, I made sure my room had an Internet connection.

The bellboy helped me up to my room on the first floor. I handed over a dollar bill to him, then entered my room, leaving my baggage at the door itself, and rushed to open my laptop bag and go online at once. I logged into Yahoo! messenger. Yes, that was the very first thing I did.

It was early morning in India and I knew she would be waiting for me.

And she really was.

We'd decided earlier that this was the time we would be on chat. Though, because I'd expected a shorter journey, I was somewhat late. And after the eight hour journey from Delhi to Heathrow, the three hours in transit, the eight hours from Heathrow to New York and the two hours, by cab, from New York to Shelton, I was severely jet-lagged.

But those twenty four hours of not being able to talk to her overrode everything else.

She was delighted to see me online. And so was I. But her delight was greater which is why she wrote so many messages in a fraction of second:

Heyyy . . . .Shona . . . you dere.
How r u . . . wen did u reach.
How was your journey?
Where are you now? You dere?
BUZZ

And I didn't reply, just asked her, 'Did u miss me?'

'Soooooo much dear. And You . . .?'

'Hmmm . . . I will let you know but first switch on your speakers and accept the voice chat request.'

I told her everything about my journey—the flights, the transit, the passengers and how I missed her amid everything. She told me how she spent her entire day without talking to me. Even her family realized how much she was missing me. Hearing each other's voice after an entire day was so . . . touching. This had never happened in the past six months. We kept talking for a long time and it was only when the electricity went off in Faridabad and her UPS, too, gave up that we finally bade goodbye.

Which was when I realized that I should take off my shoes (which I was wearing since the day before), should bring my luggage (which was still in the gallery) into my room and that, in the haste to talk to her, I had left my wallet at the reception.

Day Three
It was a Monday (OGIM—Oh God, it's Monday!). My first day at my client's office.

In the office, I first met with all my colleagues from Infosys who'd arrived onsite before me—some old faces and some new. In foreign lands, we Indians always tend to look for fellow Indians first. And I am, proudly, one such Indian.

In the next few hours, my project manager introduced me to our client and vice versa. More than their faces, I was trying to remember the way to the cafeteria, to the conference rooms and, of course, to the restrooms.

Very soon, I was occupied with my work. My weekdays passed in the office, working along with my client, meeting with different stakeholders, offshore calls and enjoying different lunches in the cafeteria. In the evenings, I used to go back to my hotel and study for the CAT. Often, I used to cook my dinner too. (To be honest, there was nothing to cook. I just heated the frozen eatables.)

But, no matter what I did, she was always on my mind.

I missed her in my US days and she missed me in her Indian nights. She missed me in her Indian days and I missed her in my US nights. Life wasn't too easy. We couldn't call each other whenever we wished. Twice a day, we were on chat: my mornings, after I woke up and before she went to bed; my nights, before I slept and after she woke up.

Day Seven
We were on chat, just like any other day, and she asked me to do something special for her.

'Shona, I want you to write me an email every day, before you sleep.

They will be with me and I will read them over and over, whenever I miss you.'

But, breaking her sweet expectation I replied, 'Hmm . . . I will try. But I don't know if I can do it after such hectic days. Office, CAT, chats, dinner . . . there is so much, you know.'

I said that not because I didn't want to write the emails, but because I wanted to give her a beautiful surprise.

I wrote a diary for her.

Somehow, I believed that handwritten words carry much more meaning and much more feeling in them. They have a special something that can't be conveyed in sterile, electronic mails. I didn't tell her about it, but at the end of every day, I started writing my feelings for her in a diary. Each and every page described how I missed her, what all I wanted to do had she been with me, wrote small verses for her. And her half-sketched picture which I drew while thinking of her, but left incomplete when I realized I was a poor artist.

Day Twelve

It was a Friday (TGIF—Thank God, it's Friday!). In the West, this day of the week is a goofy day. Officially it is a working day but, unofficially, it's anything but a working day. Though, because we were our client's vendor, our weekends started only from Friday evenings.

Enjoying these evenings, we used to hang out in bunches at the discotheques, pubs, eating joints and bowling alleys. Or we would drive down to the nearest city hosting a *desi* movie show. And *Munnabhai* was running in the US theaters too, making me recall that troubled and tender night.

Weekends, onsite, were always fun. But there was something different this time—I had to face this question from people with whom I enjoyed my weekends during my past trips.

'But you used to booze, right? So what happened now?'

I wanted to tell them the truth but didn't. The reason being, in my earlier life (I mean, before I fell in love) I used to give them *gyaan*, telling them guys should not change themselves for girls. How could I tell them that I'd left my occasional liquor for a girl? So I had to give them fake reasons.

And I'll tell you what. It's hard to give fake reasons, for two reasons. First, there's tremendous pressure from friends, especially when they are totally drunk and start swearing on each other's name to make you drink. And second, my own willingness to booze.

But I didn't.

And I was happy that I kept my promise to her.

Day Thirty

One morning—it was probably 9 o'clock—I was in my office and signed into my messenger. As usual, she had left a voice message to make my day. By now, I had a plenty of them in my voice message list. They were all so sweet that I never felt like deleting any of them. But then, when the message box got full, I had to take up the difficult task of choosing which one to delete. There was one which I could never delete, though, for it was the cutest of all. In it, she was childishly angry at me because I didn't come online one day and was yelling at me despite having a cold.

I was taking an offshore call, talking to my project team back in India, when I saw that she had come online.

'I have to show you something,' she messaged.

To which I replied, with one hand putting the speaker-phone on mute, 'I am running busy . . . You'll have to wait for a while.'

The next minute, my client manager grabbed me for a different meeting in another conference room. That day I kept rushing from one meeting to another. Some days are like that and this was that kind of day. At noon, I entered the cafeteria along with my clients for lunch and it was then that I remembered—she was waiting for me.

Damn!

I rushed back to my room and to my laptop where I checked the numerous messages she had left. The last one read, '*Kab aaoge* Shona . . . I have to show you something.'

I checked its timestamp. She wrote that an hour back. I felt bad for making her wait for me, for so many hours. Working in the afternoon shift, getting back at 11 in the night and then waiting for me for the last three hours . . . She must have been so tired, so sleepy. What did she want to show me? Had she gone? Was she asleep? Her status on the messenger appeared dormant.

I quickly fished my calling card from my wallet and dialed her number. After a few rings it got disconnected. I was trying once more when, suddenly, her message flashed on my laptop's screen, 'Was it you? R u online?'

I quickly got on the keyboard. 'Yes dear,' I wrote.

'Where were you . . . ?'

'M so so so . . . sorry dear. I am bad. I made you wait for so long . . . Actually, since morning, I am running so busy here, I completely forgot that you were online waiting for me. At least I should have told you that I might not be able to turn up . . . :-('

'This happens sometimes. I can understand.' She didn't shout at me.

'Still u know . . . But hey . . . I cannot wait for that thing you wanted to show me. Tell me what that was.'

'Can you show that to me now?' I asked her again.

And she replied, 'Yes . . . here comes the first one. Check your email.'

I refreshed my mailbox and a fresh mail from her arrived in it with a subject line that read: 1. And then came another: 2. And then, 3, 4, 5, 6, 7, 8 and 9.

Nine b-e-e-e-a-u-t-i-f-u-l photographs of her.

Amazed and spellbound by her beauty, I kept staring at those pictures. Without any doubt, those were her best pictures. They had a magical effect on me. In that moment, I struggled with two things: first, my unwillingness to take my eyes off any one picture and, second, the eagerness to see the others at the same time.

What a sweet surprise she had given me. My heart was on cloud nine knowing that this beauty was mine, and when beauty overrides your brain, you don't know what to say, you go numb with pleasure. Then, realizing that her innocent heart had sacrificed a night's sleep waiting for me, I finally typed, 'Hey Angel . . . because that's what you look like in those pictures. Thank you so much dear, for such a sweet surprise.'

Simultaneously, her message flashed on my screen, '*Achchi lag rahi hu na main*? You want to say something?'

'*Bahut!* :-* I won't be able to find better words than what I am feeling. Or maybe I will . . .'

And before I could complete my line, I heard the door of my room opening followed by footsteps. I turned back. It was my manager who was on the phone with someone and was calling me for another quick meeting. I begged his pardon for two minutes, in which I managed to say goodbye to her.

'I am still in a beautiful shock,' was my last message.

I didn't eat lunch that afternoon. The feast for my eyes satisfied my hunger.

That day onwards, one of her pictures—the only one with a close-up of hers—became my desktop's wallpaper.

Day Forty-Five
I boarded my plane back to India.

Return

It was almost midnight when I got off at Delhi airport. As soon as I was out of the immigration channel, I switched on my Indian cellphone. And I called my mom before anybody else, like she wanted, to let her know that her son was back and was absolutely fine. She too was expecting my call, and that's why she couldn't sleep (mom's are like that). I spoke to her for a few minutes and bade her goodnight. Then I moved to the conveyor belt to pick my luggage.

At the exit gate, I booked a cab to Faridabad.

No, I wasn't heading towards her but to a hotel she had booked for me. We learnt from our past mistakes that commuting between Faridabad and Delhi could be more than a little problematic. So why not book a hotel in Faridabad itself?

I was in the cab when a few SMSs made a sharp entry in my message box. All of them were from Khushi. The topmost one read:

Ur hotel is booked. Gimme
a call wen you land.

I was very eager to talk to her now that I was, once again, in her country . . . I mean our country. It's such a different feeling, returning to your beloved after a long time. Everything around you appears so lovely. Every beautiful thing brings a smile to your face. Every hour, the level of your anxiety increases as the time before you'll see each other decreases.

I called her up. Later, she told me what she did: Seeing her favorite name on the display of her phone after so long, she held her hand to her heart, smiled, closed her eyes, thanked God, took a deep breath, opened her eyes and picked up the phone.

'H-i-i-iiiiiiiiiiiii!' She jumped loudly on the ground.

'Haha . . . Helloooooooo!' I was happy to hear her crazy'hi', just like a kid.

'I am so so so happy you're back.'

'So am I.'

And we went crazy. Shouting. Laughing. Singing . . . That was how happy we were.

I heard her, going merrily around her house, letting everybody know that I was back. In a round-robin fashion, each and every lady in the house talked to me.

'*Mujhe bhi do . . . maine bhi baat karni hai.*'

'Dad is sleeping, so maybe you will be talking to him tomorrow,' she said.

Well, we kept talking till I reached my hotel. Of course, there was no reason why we shouldn't be doing that. Getting the directions from her, I explained them to the driver of my cab.

Magpie Hotel on Mathura Road was my destination for the night. It was not that good a hotel, but she had booked it because most of the good hotels in the city were full as it was the marriage season (October) and, more importantly, it was the nearest to her place.

On my way to Magpie, we were passing through the outskirts of the city and my cell was frequently losing its network coverage, and I dialed her number again and again. Before giving out completely, the network played hide and seek on

my mobile's screen for a while. I somehow managed to send
her an SMS:

Wll cal u once I
rch hotel.

To which she replied:

NO. CAL ME D MOMENT
U R GNG 2 OPEN UR ROOM.
DN'T FORGET

Well, I did what she wanted. Half an hour later, as I was
unlocking the door of my room in the hotel, I called her. We
were back on the phone when I moved into the dark room.

'Ok, now on your right hand, there is a switchboard. The
first one is the light,' she said. And I wondered why she was
instructing me.

The room was cold. The AC was on and there was a beautiful
fragrance in the room.

In the light of my cellphone's screen, I switched on the lights
of the room and what came next was a sweet surprise.

'OH MY GOD!'

In front of me was a giant bed with two bouquets of roses,
along with a note on each one of them. And they read—
'Welcome back' and 'I missed you so much.'

Apart from this, there was a tissue paper peeking out from
under the cushions. From a distance I could not read it, but
I noticed the maroon impression of her lips on it—a lovely
advance gift of love which she left for me.

I read the note.

While you were gone, I realized how badly I need you for myself.
I love you so much.

'I love you so much dear,' was the sweet reaction of my melting heart. I inhaled the scent of her kiss on that tissue and kissed it. She heard me doing that. I wanted her to hear.

The next moment, someone knocked at my door.

'Who is it?' I asked.

'Bellboy,' came the reply.

'Two minutes dear, there is some one at the door,' I told Khushi and opened the door.

'Sir, I have got water for you.'

'OK.'

He came in with a bottle of Bisleri and an upside-down glass. He kept it beside my bed and, from the corner of his eyes, he noticed all that was lying on it. Those flowers, that note. Maybe he saw the kiss too. He smiled to himself for a fraction of a second and then returned to his formal demeanor. While going back, he noticed a half-filled glass covered with a lid, along with another bottle of water.

'Oh you have already got water.'

'That's not mine. You can take it away,' I said.

As I said that, I heard her voice from the cellphone. She was shouting 'Shona! STOP HIM . . . Don't let him touch the glass . . . .'

'*RUKO!*' I shouted at the boy.

And hearing the intensity of that '*RUKO,*' he froze, just like a statue. As if, the next moment, he was about to trip a mine and I saved him. He looked at me curiously. Even I wasn't sure why she had asked me to do that.

I told him, 'I'm all good. You can leave.'

Confused, he left the room.

Closing the door from inside, I asked her why she reacted that way.

'I want you to discover that yourself,' she said. She was calm again.

While I was wondering what she meant, she asked me, 'Aren't you thirsty?'

'Maybe,' I said, removing the lid covering the glass and lifting it.

Then I heard her saying, 'You can have the water which I left in your room.'

I was about to take a sip when I realized that her sweet surprises were still coming. My heart was smiling with the delights it was receiving. There were patches of her lipstick on the circumference of that glass. Having sipped some of this water, she had left the rest for me. What a sweetheart!

'You are such a darling,' I slowly sang, enjoying the water, drinking it exactly from the spot where she had pressed her lips.

Our conversation turned romantic and we kept talking of beautiful things for quite a long time.

I think it was around 2 a.m. when we finally separated. I made her sleep, after which I went and showered. The last shower I had taken was thirty hours back, in the US.

Later that night, on my bed, surrounded by those beautiful roses, I wrote her a message:

Smhow those 45 days hv passed
bt this hiatus of few hrs to see u again
is killing me. Good nite Angel.

Unfortunately, the next morning wasn't a pleasant one.

Jet lag, change of weather, the weariness after a long journey and my night shower—all brought me down with a cold. I was sneezing, had a bad headache and an aching throat. In other words, I was completely screwed up.

In that unpleasant condition, I was turning left and right, squeezing the bouquets which I had been embracing in my sleep. It took me a long while to, finally, open my eyes completely.

Then I noticed her SMS—*Will be dere at 11.*

It was quarter to ten in my watch.

Damn! I wanted to reply asking her to come a little later. But I didn't. Rather, gathering all my energy, I got ready. I took a warm shower this time. I was slow in everything I was doing. And all that was running in my mind was: Will I get better by the time she comes here?

By eleven, I was through with my breakfast and she called me up to say that she was going to be late. She would be at my place in the next half an hour.

'OK,' I said. I kept the call short because I didn't want her to notice my condition. I was still sneezing and coughing. And someone seemed to be beating a giant drum inside my skull. The headache was killing me. I rarely get headaches, but that was one rare day. Just my luck!

For the next half an hour, weird things were running through my brain.

'Damn! Did I have to come down with a cold today, of all days?' With my running nose and a heavy, choked voice, my desire to kiss her again after forty-five days got crushed. I had been waiting for such a long time and the next day I was to fly back to Bhubaneswar. Moreover, I was not sure when I would see her next.

'What if I still kiss her?' I was still talking to myself. That one wish was debating with the germs of cold in me. But then, in the evening, I had to be at her place. What if her family noticed her sneezing and coughing, just like me? Would they figure out how I transferred my virus to their daughter? (Yes, I know, at times I think too much.)

But she reached the hotel and gave me a missed call, interrupting my weird thoughts. I rushed out of my room to receive her. And, at last, after these long one and a half months of being apart, we were standing in front of each other.

She was wearing a nice white top, blue denim (a perfect fit), a light shade of glossy lipstick and small earrings. Her hair was untied, the breeze scattering it across her face.

My beautiful was in front of me—her sneezing handsome.

Her blushes and smiles revealed how delighted she was to see me. She smiled and her eyes revealed her satisfaction of being with me again. And within me I was all happy, excited and nervous.

'Hi,' I said, giving her a small (or maybe the smallest) hug. I did that with the fear of others noticing, though there was no one outside. There was a little hesitation in the initial moments. It happens, you know . . . And with that 'Hi,' she realized my condition immediately.

'Cold *hua hai tumhe*?' she asked, raising her eyebrows.

'*Nah* . . . It's just a little thing,' I answered as if I was fine.

'But . . .' And she kept looking at me, trying to help me. 'You want to take some medicine?'

'No . . . no. It's okay, dear. I will be all right . . . Just because of the climate change. But I will be fine soon. Now shall we move in or are we going to stand here for the rest of the day?' I said.

The worry on her face turned into a little smile. (A fake one—she was still worried.)

We went to my room. She said I should have some tea in order to help my cold, so I ordered a cup of it for myself and a soft drink for her. (Nobody in her family drinks tea, remember? Strange family.)

Her physical presence in front of me after such a long time was making me conscious. I don't know why, at times, I get into that mode. And in these blank conditions I always need some time to get into a comfort zone. But the feeling inside me was good. To see her, to sit beside her, touch her again . . . . But, all this without inhaling her fragrance. (Blocked noses can't smell.)

But that short tea-time (my teatime and her soft-drink time) helped me feel better, physically, allowing me time to become comfortable in her company.

A few minutes later, I was telling her the stories of my onsite trip, discussing official things, laughing at stupid ones, watching the pictures I had taken in the US, on my laptop. In no time, on that giant bed, we were lying on our stomachs, next to each other, our feet paddling in the air above us, our hands underneath our chins and our eyes on the screen of the laptop. We were watching those short movies I had shot on my trip. And beside us, were those flowers with which I slept the night before, her notes and the tissue carrying her kiss's imprint which was now making her shy. She was acting as if she never noticed that on my bed.

With my cold, I didn't feel like roaming around the malls of Faridabad, so we had to cancel her plan. Rather, we stayed back in our room. We discussed some important things. Like, when should our parents meet? What time will it be good for us to get married? Where should we settle down after marriage, taking our careers into consideration?

And I remember well, on that last question she quickly responded, 'It should be Delhi.'

'But why not Bhubaneswar?' I calmly revolted back.

And like a five-year-old kid, she answered, full of innocence, 'It will be hard for me to live far away from my Mumma.'

Stroking her forehead and hair, I said, 'We will bring your mom for you, in dowry.'

And we laughed.

During our conversation that day, we took a U-turn to discuss our respective pasts. Our college life, our school friends and our family. The sweet memories and the hard times. And on one occasion, she burst into tears. She happened to recall some things in her life which she could never share with anyone else but me. Taking her in my arms, I wiped her tears. She said she felt relieved after sharing that with me, and she made me promise that I would never tell it to anyone. And promises . . . Promises are meant to be kept.

I held her head on my shoulder, rubbing her back gently, drying her moist eyes. She felt good and rested in my arms for quite some time.

In order to change her mood I started telling her some jokes, just to comfort her. And when I saw that smile returning to her face I said, 'Hmm . . . So let us see what I have got from the US for my dearest . . .'

'*Sachhi?*'

'*Muchhi,*' I said and jumped out of my bed to unlock my bag. She also followed me and, while I was opening it, she stood behind me, looking over my shoulder. I quickly recalled something and turned back to say, 'Girls are not allowed to stare in guys' bags.'

She laughed, but fought back to stand there and check my bag along with me. Seeing the big polythene bag I took out, her smile widened. But when she reached for it, I grabbed it back.

'A . . . a . . . aa! Not like this. Let me open it and show you.'

'Ok.'

And I pulled out a purple top with short sleeves, along with a matching pastel-coloured skirt.

'Wow!' she stared at the dress open-mouthed. 'This is awesome!' (Girls love surprises. No?)

'Not yet,' I said. 'For it to be really awesome, it needs to be on you. Wear it and show me.' I pointed to the washroom, where she could go and change. Carrying a smile and that dress she walked away.

Back in that room, I crossed my fingers. I had never bought anything of that sort, ever, for any girl. I didn't have a sister, nor did I have any prior girlfriend with whom I could have learnt something about buying clothes for girls.

A few minutes later, I heard the washroom door getting unlocked. She popped her head out first and asked, 'Shall I come out?'

'Please! I am dying,' I said.

'1 . . . 2 . . . 3 . . .' She counted before coming out. And then, she was in front of me. Seeing her, I uncrossed my fingers with immense pleasure. She looked stunning in my gift.

'B-e-a-u-t-i-f-u-l!'

And, suddenly, I turned my gaze away from her, thinking that my looking at her that way should not bring her bad luck. But then, I looked at her again—I couldn't resist.

That top and the skirt suited her body so well, as if they had been made just for her. I was surprised and, silently, I congratulated myself. Even she was surprised and, probably, that's why she said, 'I never knew you know me so well.'

That dress . . . or, should I say her beautiful body-line was complementing the dress. Looking at herself in the mirror of my room, she said 'I look my best in this dress. This is the best one I will have in my wardrobe.'

'Then promise me.'

'What?'

'That this one will only be worn by you and no one else . . . Not even your sisters. I want to see this only on you.'

'I promise.'

And with that promise she realized that she was getting late. I helped her pack her gifts in a polythene bag after which she hugged me and said, 'It's beautiful being with you after so long.'

'Same here.'

At the door she explained the way to reach her home. I was to visit her family again.

'Don't be late.' She said and waved me good-bye and left.

I was walking down to her place in the evening. I think I was two blocks away from her house when I saw two people walking in my direction. One was about three years old, and holding his hand was a man of about sixty. I thought I knew who they were.

Seeing me, the old man halted.

The little kid tried to pull him along. '*Chalo!* Ice Cream!' he screamed. The poor kid tried his best but failed.

I looked at the person in front of me and the old man raised his finger, a few lines appeared on his forehead. He was wondering if I was their guest for the evening.

But before he could speak, I said, 'I think I am coming to your place. Am I right?'

'Ravin?'

'*Haanji.*' I smiled and touched his feet.

He was Khushi's dad and the kid was Daan who was pulling his grandfather to the nearest ice-cream parlor.

But now, the cute kid held my hand and shouted on the street asking me, '*Aap Khushi maasi ke dost ho . . . hain . . . aap ho na?*'

I bent down and kissed his small hands, saying, '*Haha . . . hmm.*'

Soon he forgot all about the ice-cream and started pulling me towards his house. All the while, he kept shouting, '*Aao na . . . Maasi aapke liye tayaar ho rahi hai . . . Aao . . . Aao.*'

He kept pulling me till I entered their house. In no time, I found myself surrounded by Mumma, Neeru and Misha di (Daan's mother). Everybody was laughing at the way Daan was dragging me. I slipped my fingers out of Daan's grip to greet everyone.

Later, we all settled down in the drawing room. Khushi's dad was also back and had joined us.

The questions started—The kind of how-was-your-journey-and-ifeverything-is-fine types.

And answering them all I managed to make my space amid all of them.

Meanwhile, Khushi too appeared.

The rounds of snacks started, exactly like last time. Of all her family, it was her dad whom I talked to most. He was trying to understand what exactly I did, being a software engineer. In turn, he was also explaining what he used to do as an engineer in the Indian Air Force. (Impressive!)

Later on, he brought up the subject of marriage too, indirectly—how and when Misha di got married and then Ami di and now it was

Khushi's turn. He also talked about his married daughters' in-laws, their family and their professions (though I knew everything in detail).

I wondered what the purpose was. I recalled that ad in which a guy's would-be father-in-law asks him, 'You are going to marry my daughter. But will you be able to support a family?' To which I answered, in my mind, 'I think, in marriage, I will only take your daughter along with me. The rest of your family, you will have to manage on your own.'

But, jokes apart, I found her dad to be a real sensible and understanding person. I liked his personality as well.

We all were waiting for Deepu (Khushi's brother) who was driving back home. Mumma was getting impatient and kept calling him up, checking how far he was from home.

Little Daan was adding to the flavor of our conversation every now and then, making everybody laugh with his childish pranks. He was on my lap when, suddenly, he reacted to a car's horn and rushed to the door. It was Deepu. Minutes later, he pulled Deepu into the drawing room, just like he had brought me. I shook hands with Deepu and he joined us.

He seemed to be the most robust person in their entire family, with a wide chest, broad shoulders and a well-built physique.

He was working with some oil wells in Assam and had come back on holiday. So now, from my job the conversation shifted to his.

We sat in the drawing room for a long time and at around 8.30, we had our dinner.

After our meal, Khushi took me to the other side of their house to show me the garden, the money plant and the guava trees which she used to climb sometimes, picking guavas for her mom. Well, I could have got a little privacy with her but Neeru and Mumma didn't leave us alone.

The evening at their home passed quite well. By then I had met the people whom I didn't see the last time—her dad, Deepu, Misha di and cute Daan. I was happy that I was going to be part of a nice family. (And I assume they were happy too!)

By 9.30, I was all set to leave for my hotel.

'I think I should make a move before I get too late,' I said to the people around me, but especially her Dad.

'Hmm . . . Yes, you are at a new place. It's better if you reach your hotel well in time. Deepu will drop you,' he said looking at Deepu, whom Daan was punching, the way he had seen his favorite WWF fighters doing.

After a short while, Deepu was starting his car and I was bidding everyone goodbye. Daan kept shouting, '*Mujhe bhi jaana hai . . . Mujhe bhi jaana hai!*' And before he could make a scene, his mother allowed him to get in the car.

Amid all this, I looked at Khushi, silently asking her if she too could come. And I think Mumma noticed my look. Maybe that's why she told Khushi, '*Tu bhi saath mein chali jaa . . .*'

Her dad was probably going to interrupt her, but I changed the topic as soon as I heard her mother giving her a green signal. In a short while, we were in the back-seat of the car. Daan kept shuffling places between her and me. In those last minutes of being together, we held hands but didn't talk much.

Soon we were going to be apart again, for an uncertain amount of time.

We reached Magpie a bit too quickly, and it was time to say goodbye.

Deepu came out of the car and he took Daan's hand in his. I shook hands with him and gave a kiss to Daan, who asked me when I would come again, and told me that I should not forget to get chocolates for him.

Now was the turn of my sweetheart. She stood beside the car. I looked in her eyes. They were expressing the same feelings which mine were. She came and stood right in front of me. I couldn't say anything but smiled sadly. That one moment, she didn't care about Deepu's presence but kept looking into my eyes. Taking Daan inside the car, Deepu started the vehicle to let his sister know they were supposed to get back.

She ignored that too and came closer to me and said, 'I want to be yours, forever.'

'You are mine. A little more than forever,' I said.

And we hugged each other this time without caring about the world around us.

Then she sat in the car. I kept waving to her till the car turned out of the hotel's gate.

Back in Bhubaneswar, life got back on the same track. Office, phone calls to her, gym, phone calls to her, CAT preparation, phone calls to her. But what was different this time was that I had started relating her voice to her appearance, her body language, her fragrance.

Days passed and our desire to be together kept increasing with each day.

It was Diwali and, in the evening, our entire veranda was shining with the sparkle of *diyas* and candles and crackers. With one hand, I was shooting everything happening at my place with my camera; in the other hand, I was carrying my cell, talking to Khushi. We were telling each other about the atmosphere at our respective places. The phones on both sides were shuffling through different hands. First, it was me talking to her, then my mom and her, then her mom and me, then my mom and hers, then she and I again, then me and her sister . . . he, she, she, me . . . everybody. But each one of them mentioned this: She would be celebrating her next Diwali as part of our family.

A few more days of our life passed.

Life returned to its best after we were released from our vow of not talking to each other after 10 p.m. on weekdays. Yes, CAT was over. It went well for both of us. (Everyone has the right to say 'It went well,' till the results are out!) But yes, the completion of CAT marked the beginning of our best days. Well, actually it was nights. December, January. Winter. Cold nights, blankets and, wrapped in those warm blankets, our cellphones and us. (I tell you—winter is the most romantic time. And so are rainy days. And . . . and . . . and, wait a minute, summer too! Am I getting something wrong? Or, maybe, it's that every season brings a different flavor if you are in love.)

One night, it was 12.10 a.m. and we had left the year 2006 behind, and 2007 was ten minutes young for us. Despite the overloaded telephone network, somehow we were among the lucky ones to get connected. Of course, we had to try a hundred times to call each other.

She was the first one to reach me and do you know what her first words were? No, she didn't wish me a happy new year. Instead, she shouted with happiness, 'Shona! We are getting married this year. 2007 has arrived. Wow!'

Time and again, all these little things (which, for me, were big things) she did would make me feel, more and more, that I would never be able to live without her.

'Yes! We will marry this year and then we'll live together. Happy new year, dear,' I wished her.

'A very happy new year to you too.'

Network congestion that night did not allow us to talk much. Still, we were satisfied enough. And we felt that, just like us, there must have been so many couples dying to talk to each other. Who knows, maybe some among them were going to get married the same year . . .

Apparently, my love story overrode my friendship. This should not have been the case. But, this was the case. After a long time, it was Amardeep who connected Happy, MP and me with an e-mail. In his e-mail, he had taken a screenshot of MP's and my profile on Shaadi.com. His first intention was to mock at us for the exaggerated information we had provided about ourselves on this website. Secondly, he wanted to know if this website happened to work for us.

Later, that evening, all four of us got together on a chat conference.

Happy: Raam ji, so finally u caught these a★★★-holes haan!! Good job.

Amardeep: Ha ha ha . . . they were playing smart, without letting us know nything.

Amardeep: Now speak up u two. Wat hv u managed to gt till now?

Ravin: If u hv searched our profile, den surely u too wud be having one. Bataa saaley?

Amardeep: If I will have, I won't hide it. Now don't change the topic. MP you tell.

Happy: Yeah, MP tell us . . . how many till now J????????

MP: Arey yaar . . . it was long time back. Nothing serious. I hardly check it now a days.

Amardeep: Achha!! That's why your activity percentage on this site (as it shows) is 98% J.

Ravin: Ha ha ha. Gaatch u!!

Amardeep: Y d hell are u laughing so much Ravin? U tell . . . wat hv u got?

Ravin: Well! I have got something.

MP: Got what????????

Ravin: Her.

Happy: Whom?

Ravin: Her name is Khushi.

Amardeep: R u serious?

Ravin: Damn serious.

Happy: Hu . . . Huuuuuuuuuuuuu. He gaat it!!!!!! . . . he gaat it!!!!!!!!!!!!!!!!!!!! This gonna be f★★★in interesting. Everybody: Leave this text chat and turn your headphones ON. We gonna listen to his story right now.

And, for the next half hour, I had to narrate my so-far story to them. The conversation ended with a celebration of loud noises, best wishes and the promise to make them all talk to her soon.

8 January 2007

My not-so-good-looking house was looking better that morning. And why not? The first would-be in-laws of that house were to come that day—Khushi's mom and dad.

Understanding the fact that my Mumma couldn't travel in winters because of her asthma, they had agreed to come down to our place.

I was there at Sambalpur station to receive them. The train arrived on time and I could easily trace them in the crowd, getting down at the station. I touched their feet, welcomed them and picked up their bags. On our way back from the station, I showed them certain landmarks in my small hometown. The longest dam—Hirakud—built on the river Mahanadi. Her Mumma was astonished when I told her that it was 4.8 kilometers long. To which she mischievously replied by boasting about the Bhakra Nangal dam (the highest one) which she had seen.

By 12.30 that afternoon we reached home. Her parents were welcomed by mine. Both the moms and both the dads were happy to finally see each other. Well, in our country, seeing the boy is one of the most important steps in the entire marriage process, but true happiness comes to the parents when they hug each other with those smiling faces. I think this bolsters their trust and confidence in each other's family, allowing them to go ahead with this thing called marriage. I still doubt that they really trust us youngsters one hundred percent.

But anyway, the folks got introduced to each other. Except for Tinku, who was in Bhubaneswar for his weekend support at his office, they had seen my entire family.

We all then moved to the guest room where her parent's would stay. They liked our place, especially her mom, who noticed the guava and the *jamun* tree in our courtyard. And this time it was me who boasted, 'See, our tree is bigger than yours.' And everybody laughed.

While they enjoyed their lemon squash, my mom returned to her kitchen. She was very busy. In a short while they were given some privacy, to get comfortable in the new place, relax a bit and take a shower. We all then met at lunch.

Of course it had to be good. And it was, actually, one of the best luncheon gatherings at my place—a good menu, good people, good conversation and all that for a good purpose. Along with the meal, the elderly people went down memory lane, recalling marriages in their period and comparing it with the present system. And I wondered if, forty years later, I would be recalling the present marriage system. Or maybe, who knows, marriage might not even exist by then . . .

Apart from that, there were a lot of things they discussed: the current society, mind-sets, the generation-gap fundas and all that. And I had to agree with whatever they said, though there were a lot of things I would have revolted against. But then, all I was bothered about was my marriage to their daughter. So I nodded my head to whatever they said about our young generation's failings. But thankfully they ended on a happy note, saying that we are the bright future of this country. (And I said to myself, 'Oh, thank you so much, folks! I am honored.')

Being a good child, I gave the required privacy to the parents, so that they could discuss what they had come to discuss. I went out to the veranda and lying on a cot underneath the *jamun* tree, I called her up.

'Heyyyyyyyy!'

'Hiiiiiiiiiiiiiiiiiiii!'

'What's up there?' she asked.

'The sky,' I answered.

'Shut up! *Batao naa*. How's my mom? Is she fine?'

'*Kamaal hai*. At least ask me how *I* am first!'

'Nothing's going to happen to you. You'll always be fine because I'm in your life,' she replied sweetly, though I wondered—didn't the same apply to her mother as well?

'Your mom is doing very good *aur haan* your dad is also fine,' I added that taunt to make her realize that she should have asked about her dad too. But she always said she is her mom's daughter first . . . Her dearest daughter.

Then I told her all that had happened, so far, at my place and the agenda for the rest of the evening. Meanwhile, there was a burst of laughter from inside and I thought I should go back and check on the things being discussed. We hung up and I went back in.

I'd left them alone to plan my marriage but, damn! the old folks were cracking jokes, recalling the funny things I used to do when I was a kid. Why do parents have to reveal all those embarrassing secrets to others? I was not the only kid in the world to suck his thumb in his sleep! What's the big deal?

But anyway . . .

We made a plan for the evening—a visit to Hirakud dam. Mom wanted to stay back home, because of her health and to take care of other household chores, most importantly, dinner. I wanted to stay back with mom but she wanted me to be with them. It was just a matter of half an hour or so and we would be back, she said.

So after an hour's nap and evening tea, we went ahead with the plan. As our destination was only three kilometers from our house, it didn't take us much time and we reached there in ten minutes.

We parked our vehicles and then climbed the *Jawahar Minaar* tower (the tallest building there) which was built to keep vigil. We were almost 150 feet above the ground and, from there, the catchment area of the dam appeared at its best. On our right was the giant structure of the dam—those hovering pulleys, the noise of the turbine coming from some place far below, the big water reservoir behind the wall and the tributaries of water originating and passing by my town towards the east. On our left was the scenic horizon, with half of the burning sun above it, creating a mesmerizing sunset, giving us a hint to interpret the common line between the sky and the water.

Very soon, our shadows perched in the longer shadow of the tower were fading. The sun was bidding goodbye for the day. And there stood those silent islands, big and small, far and near, in the miles and miles of water, waiting for the night-creatures to come out and rule them. Birds were flying back to their homes and, from that tower, we could see the lights in our town coming on. Everyone there appreciated the beauty of the place.

I was happy I had brought Khushi's mom and dad there. And I remember very well what her Mumma said. 'When Khushi comes here, bring her to this place. She'll love it.' And her dad said, 'It was a similar, spellbinding, scenic view which made me write a poem when I passed through the Khandala Hills on the Pune–Mumbai expressway. And I have the same urge now.'

That was so good to hear. I don't know if he wrote any poem on it or not. But they didn't know, till then, that my small town, Burla, had such beauty in its lap. And, on that note, we were on our way back home, the setting sun colouring us with its hues and thanking the 'guests' for their visit to this natural heaven.

We were back at around 8 p.m., a little before dinner. And this is when people actually started discussing the purpose for which Khushi's parents were here. And, being a good lover-boy, I was updating my beloved about the proceedings at our premises. Moments later, when I joined the discussion, we all arrived at a common decision.

The ring-ceremony was to be held in Faridabad, on 14 February 2007.

Khushi and I had chosen this date long ago. She had said she wanted to celebrate this Valentine's Day with her fiancé (the future me), whereas my stand was that I wanted to celebrate this day with my girlfriend (the current she). So we both agreed to exchange our rings on the evening of 14 February. For the first half of the day she would be my girlfriend and for the later half, I would be her fiancé. Such a simple solution, no?

So, the ring-ceremony would be on 14 February. And the marriage, some time in November.

After that, we had our dinner, and then her parents went to their room, quite happily. My parents and I had a brief discussion, planning some of the things at a personal level, especially for the engagement which was a month later.

~

She is differently happy today. It seems she wants to tell me something. And I am asking—What? But she is taking her sweet time. I hear her turning the pages of newspaper. Then she speaks up.

'Shona!' *And after a moment of silence she adds,* 'Your promise to me about that boozing thing . . .'

'Hmm . . .'

'I want to set you free from that promise.'

'What?' *For a moment, I cannot figure out the context. But, still, I am happy. I again hear the sound of newspaper pages.*

She says, 'You kept your promise for the past seven months. I'm sure alcohol won't turn you bad.'

I doubt that's the only reason and ask her again, 'Are you sure? Is this the only reason?'

Mischievously, she reveals the whole truth. She reads out an article from the newspaper which describes the various positive aspects of limited alcohol intake. It also says that a couple can make their romantic moments special with a glass of champagne.

I am smiling.

She says, 'I respect you for keeping your promise to me till the day I ask you to break it.'

I don't say anything, but I smile. I am feeling nice about this.

She says 'It's been a long time for you. Do you feel like enjoying a drink with your friends tonight?'

'No.'

'Why?'

'Haha . . . Well, not tonight.' *I am laughing.* 'I am glad that you are setting me free from this promise and I am happier that I could keep it. I only booze in order to give company to my friends. Maybe the next time they want me to, I will be able to drink with them. I am in no hurry, though.'

She says she feels so comfortable with my last line.

~

It was Friday afternoon and, as usual, I called her up before lunch. I had to tell her that we had made our reservations and also when we'd be arriving at her place. And I wanted to know what all was happening at their end. Actually, I already had an idea; still, all these things related to our engagement were so beautiful that we loved to talk about them again and again. It happens with everyone, no?

'Hey.'

'Heyyy! Hi, my cute baby.'

'Listen, I have completed my next task too. We have got our . . .'

But she interrupted me to say, '*Arey,* wait. I'll tell you about my task.' She seemed very excited and, of course, completely ignored what I was saying. She was very happy. I mean she is usually happy, but that afternoon she was differently happy.

I heard her jump off her bed onto the floor.

'Give me a second,' she said and started singing to herself. La la . . . Lalala . . . La la.

'Weird,' I thought and waited for her one second to complete.

'Ok! Do you know what I have done?' she asked in her cutest voice.

'Hmm . . . No. Tell me.'

'I have just painted some flower vases. And some candle pots, you know the kind? Bowl-shaped earthen pots which will be filled with water, and fresh rose petals and a few small, lighted candles will be floating on the surface.'

'Wow! But what are you going to do with this?'

'*Arey buddhu!* We will place them on the podium where we will be exchanging our rings that evening. To add an aesthetic touch and sweet fragrance to the surroundings.'

'Oh . . . Wow! Nice *yaar*, this will be awesome.'

Then she got busy again. Probably working again on those candle pots.

'*Achcha,* listen. I have made the reservations,' I tried again to tell her.

'Wow! You know what? I have made an awesome design on it. It's looking good . . . It's looking so beautiful!'

I don't know what had happened to her. She was completely ignoring me and enjoying her preparation for her engagement evening. She was singing, she was laughing more than I ever heard her, she thought everything around her was so beautiful.

La . . . La la . . . La la . . . Laa . . .

'Heyyyyyyy you know what? The entire menu is selected. Yes! I've done that. And dad has given the order accordingly. Everything is purchased apart from small accessories. I will buy them tomorrow.' And she kept narrating her entire list, what she was going to buy and wear on the engagement.

'*Arey, dekthe reh jaaoge*. In that first look, I'll take your breath away.' she started jumping and singing again, this time at a higher pitch.

'What's happened to you?' I heard her mother ask.

'She's gone mad,' I heard Neeru say.

And Khushi? She kept laughing and dancing.

'*Arey*, Mumma, I am going crazy . . . . coz . . . coz . . . three days later,

IT'S MY ENGAGEMENT!'

La . . . La la . . . La la . . . Laa . . .

And then, I think, she made her mother dance with her. She was crazy. The madness of being in love . . . Her dream coming true with every passing day . . . She was on cloud nine.

All of a sudden, her mother took the phone to talk to me.

'My daughter's gone completely mad today . . . She's been laughing all morning. She's so happy, I've started worrying . . . *kahin kuch . . .*'

'When you were getting married you must have felt the same!' I heard Khushi shouting in the background, her voice fading away as if she was going out of the room.

'Did you hear?' her innocent and worried mother asked.

'Haha. But Mumma, today I like your daughter even more. You don't worry. Just let her enjoy the preparations.'

From her mother I found out that, since morning, she had been trying on her dress for that evening every now and then, her sandals, her bangles. She had not even eaten breakfast in her excitement. All morning her hands were dipped in the paint she was applying to those vases and candle pots.

'Do you want to talk to Ravin?' her mother asked her.

And from outside came her faint, childish, arrogant voice, 'Mumma, tell him I am busy planning my engagement, so don't disturb me.'

She was so lost in the euphoria of her engagement that she probably forgot the person whom she was getting engaged to!

I left my cute princess to her work. But before I hung up, I let her mother know about our reservations and the time when we'd be arriving at Faridabad. And I heard Khushi's, 'La . . . La . . . Laaaaa . . .'

I was wondering how she was handling all this. On one hand, I was struggling to get everything completed for the ceremony. My life was screwed up: booking tickets, calling and planning all my friends' schedules, buying clothes and jewelry. And shopping for all the 'miscellaneous' things—which was the biggest headache of all. I was tired. I was frustrated. On the other hand, Khushi was handling all this so easily. Laughing, kidding, enjoying each and every second. Planning, shopping and trying everything on, one more time. I envied her for being so relaxed amid all this. And I loved her for this very reason.

Done with my lunch, alone in the food-court of my office that afternoon, I was laughing recalling her euphoria. I felt happy for her and for myself for having her in my life.

Khushi's funda of life was so simple, yet fruitful—she wanted to live and enjoy every moment of her life. She kept saying, 'Forget what others think when you wish to dance in the rain. Just do it. It's your moment. It's your happiness.' She was correct when she said engagements, marriages, love (or, to be precise, *first* love)—all these are one-time occasions. Therefore, they are precious. You have to celebrate them. You have to make them memorable.

Thinking of all this even I wanted to act crazy. 'Yes! It's my engagement,' I said to myself in excitement. And with a last sip of water I returned to my office to complete the leftover tasks, before I went on leave.

I filled in my leave form, for the next two weeks, on my computer. In the 'reason' section of the form, I wrote, 'It's my engagement! My cell won't be reachable for any code fixes or test reports, but only for your good wishes.'

Later that night, I was feeling this excitement creating waves in me. Soon I would be engaged. I would be called somebody's fiancé. The freedom of being with my friends and staring at other girls may be gone. That one ring, which I would soon be wearing on my finger, would stop all incoming traffic of other girls. My bachelorhood was going to expire soon . . .

Would I enjoy my life going forward, just the way I did till now? I didn't know. But I wanted that ring on my finger. I couldn't wait any longer. I didn't know the future but, yes, I wanted to marry Khushi. I was dying to. All of a sudden, I wanted to have her with me. I wanted to stare at her, kiss her, love her. Ripples of romance were making troughs and crests in the ocean of my heart. I called her up.

The moment she picked up the phone I said, 'I think I want to make love to you.'

'Hmm? Haha. You're nuts. I am in my office and have high-priority defects to be assigned for closure,' she answered with a naughty laugh.

A few weeks back, she had moved to a US project and was working night-shifts. I knew that but I was so lost in my thoughts, I kept talking. '. . . And I want to close my eyes and feel your face with my fingers . . .'

'Hey! Shona . . . Listen,' she was still laughing, trying to halt my thought process.

'. . . And then my fingers . . .'

'Listen dear! Pleaseeeeeeeeeee. I understand your mood. But, I have some very urgent tasks,' she said gently, so that I would not get hurt.

'Screw work, screw defects,' I said.

'I love you dear. But this is my last day at office, before I take leave. Don't you want me to complete all my work here so that I can enjoy my own engagement?'

This is how she always made me think and brought me back to reality.

'Hmmm . . .' I said, to let her know I understood but, still, was disappointed.

'I promise, I will wake you up at around five in the morning, as soon as I reach home,' she quickly said to comfort me.

'Wake me up at five. Why?'

'Mmm . . . Maybe I'll want to feel your fingers on my face . . .'

'Gotcha! Enjoy working.'

'Enjoy your sleep before an erotic morning. See you at five.'

She kissed me and returned to her 'high-priority defects'.

Half asleep, I reached for my cell underneath my pillow. From the faint light coming in through the curtains, I could make out it was morning. I checked the time on the screen of my phone. It was 6.30 a.m.

I remembered Khushi was supposed to call me. Why didn't she call? Did she fall asleep? Still in the mood to continue last night's interrupted conversation, I dialed her number. I was still under my blanket on that chilly morning. For a long, romantic chat, I put on my hands-free and closed my eyes before I entered a world of romance with her.

Her phone kept ringing but she didn't pick it up.

'I won't let you sleep dear,' I murmured to myself and redialed.

To my surprise I heard a male voice. 'Hello?' The voice was breathing heavily.

'Who is this?' I asked, suddenly awake.

'Girish.'

I could make out he was rushing somewhere. There were noises around him.

'Why do you have Khushi's cell?'

He didn't answer but handed the cell to someone else.

'Hello,' said another male voice.

'Pushkar?'

'Yes, Ravin.'

'What's up, *yaar*? All you people? Where is Khushi?' I asked anxiously, throwing off the blanket.

'Ravin, we are rushing to the ICU. Khushi met with an accident.'

The Unexpected

'W-H-A-T-?' Something struck my heart. I jumped off my bed. 'ACCIDENT?' I rechecked.

'While coming back from office, her cab met with an accident . . .'

My heartbeats increased. Pushkar then rushed off to see someone, probably a doctor and passed that call back to Girish.

'Girish, tell me the truth. What has happened to her? Is she all right?'

He was silent.

'Speak up! Goddammit. She is fine *na*?' I shouted at him. I could feel my feet shaking, losing their grip on ground. And I started rushing here and there in my room.

'I don't know, Ravin.'

'What do you mean you don't know?'

He answered softly. 'The cab got hit by some giant truck. The driver . . . the driver . . . he . . .'

'What happened?'

'He died on the spot.'

'Oh God!' That scared the hell out of me. 'Girish. For heaven's sake tell me about Khushi. Please Girish . . . Please.'

'Khushi is in the ICU. The doctor's haven't confirmed anything. She has suffered a lot of blood loss . . . .'

I started screaming.

'Was there anyone else in the cab?' I further asked.

'Yes, one more guy, who was sitting next to the driver. But he is fine. He has gotten some minor scratches. The car was completely smashed from the right side, leading to the fatal injuries to the driver on the front and Khushi who was sitting just behind the driver.' Girish replied.

Moments later, Pushkar returned and comforted me, saying that the doctors were taking care of her and they felt they would be able to get the situation under control.

'All of us are here, Ravin. Don't panic. She will be all right. The doctors are positive. I have just talked to them.'

'Yes, Pushkar. She will be fine. I am sure she will be. She *has* to be,' I whispered, praying that my words would come true.

'Listen, I will call you up soon to update you on her condition. Right now I have to go and check out her medicines and other things.'

'Yeah . . . yeah . . . ya . . . You just go ahead with what's required. I'll . . . I'll wait for your call.'

Back in my room, I was still in shock, wondering if all that was real or just a nightmare and that when I woke up I would find Khushi was well.

But, unfortunately, it was real.

I felt suffocated. I was trying to breathe in as much air as possible. I opened all the windows, trying to make contact with the world outside my home. I was alone in my house. And that terrible shock was tearing at me in my loneliness. I called up my parents but disconnected the call before anyone took it, wondering how to give them this news. I wanted to get a grip on myself first. So many fears crowded my mind. I didn't know what to do, so I rushed to the other room, to my worship-place. With my hands joined, I said to God, 'No! Don't make these bad thoughts come true. Please God. Not her. PLEASE.'

Later that morning, I called my family to tell them. They did not believe what they heard first, but later helped me, saying she will be fine. I told them I was going to book the next available flight. For the rest of the day, I kept calling her family members. I was restless. I got my flight confirmed.

Before the day ended, I wrote an SMS and forwarded it to all my friends who were about to attend my ring ceremony.

Friends, there is bad news.
Khushi has met with an accident
and everything else stands postponed.

The next morning, I got up from my bed at around 6.30 though I had been awake since 5, struggling to get rid of all bad thoughts.

I went to my closet, opened it and, then, with my palms joined and eyes closed, I bowed my head in front of Guru Nanak's picture which I kept on the first shelf. In my heart, I uttered, 'Heal her wounds and make her well . . . Please! I know you can do that.'

I stood there for a while. A little later, I opened my eyes, looked up and walked away, leaving the closet door open. On my way to the bathroom, I halted to see myself in the mirror beside my computer table. I looked scared and pale. A tear was still on my right eyelash. I wiped it off and, taking a deep breath and putting on a false smile, I said to the mirror, 'Your sweetheart will be all right. She is such a sweet girl. God cannot be so cruel that He'll harm her any more.' Saying that to myself, I rushed to the bathroom as I was getting late for my flight.

By 7.30 I was through with my bath. There was an hour left for me to get ready. Whatever I was doing, there were two names always on my lips: 'Khushi' and 'God'.

I went to the closet, picked up my prayer book and then sat on my cot with my legs crossed. For the next ten minutes, I prayed with utmost devotion and concentration. There was pin-drop silence in my room. In my prayer, I again begged God to save my Khushi and get her out of danger. With this, I bowed my head in front of the prayer book, wrapped it in its bag and kept it back in the closet with utmost care. Saying my prayer every morning had been my daily routine since college and, probably, today, I was subconsciously demanding the results of my prayers.

I did not feel like having breakfast. How could I, when my beloved was unconscious in the ICU? I skipped it and left for the airport.

Outside, the bright sun was wishing good morning to Bhubaneswar. And I was desperate to get some good news about Khushi. Every now and then, I was checking my cell for any missed call or SMS. Early on Sunday, the roads were not crowded. I hailed an auto-rickshaw and without bargaining, for the first time in my life, I got in with my airbag.

'Where?' asked the auto-rickshaw driver.

'Airport.'

By 9.30, I was at the airport. I got my bag checked in. There were still some twenty minutes left before my flight. I could not resist calling up someone in Faridabad to get an update on Khushi's condition. I dialed her number. Someone picked up the phone.

'Hello,' said a feminine voice.

'Hi! Misha di.' By now I could recognize the voices of everyone in Khushi's family.

'Hi, Ravin. How are you?'

'I am Ok didi, how are you? And any update from the hospital?'

'The doctors have not attended to her this morning. They'll probably give an update by eleven.'

I was getting restless, not knowing Khushi's condition.

Misha di then asked, 'When will you be reaching here?'

'Right now I'm at the airport and my flight is going to depart in a few minutes. So, probably by one in the afternoon . . . I think the security check has started. I'll have to hang up. Will see you guys when I reach there.'

'Yes, yes. You go on. Reach here safely and then we will talk. Bye.'

'Bye,' I said and went to the security check.

A little later, I was in the aircraft, on my seat, trying to cheer myself up with the fact that I got a window-seat. But, in no time, I was worried again. I was lost in a series of thoughts, when a beautiful hand offered me some candies.

'May I offer you some candies, sir?' the air hostess asked.

'No thanks.'

Even her lovely face could not get me to say yes. Maybe because no one appeared as beautiful to me, any more, as my own Khushi. And at that very moment, a thought flashed through my brain: 'Once you fall in love, things like external beauty, apparel and so on become unimportant.'

The thought surprised me. I wondered if this was what we call the magic of being in love.

Whatever it was, but at that time I was sure about one thing—that I did not like myself in this mood at all. I mean, just the day before, I was so happy to see my blazer, her engagement ring and her *sari*. Look at me now. 'Hey Ravin! You have to get out of this mood. This is absolutely not you,' I said to myself.

By now, the aircraft, the passengers and those air hostesses were all in the air. I looked outside the window, observing the white clouds and those birds we passed by, a few seconds back. I wondered how long it would have taken me to go to Faridabad for weekend dates with Khushi, if I were a bird. I had almost lost myself in those happy thoughts, when the fat lady sitting beside me asked me to shutter the window because of the scorching sun. I don't know how the sunrays could have made her skin any darker. But anyway, I was not in the mood for an argument and I did what she wanted.

It was time for lunch now. I realized this when I saw the food trolley in the aisle. But I wasn't feeling hungry. I was very sad, wondering how such a day had come. And, at the same moment, I knew that if I dwelt on these thoughts, the journey would be very hard for me. I made up my mind to have at least a sandwich and drive my mind away from those bad thoughts. 'Think of something interesting or funny. Oh! How about planning a sequence of *bhangra* steps for the engagement night?' I said to myself. Then had to add, 'Which will now be postponed by a few months . . .'

By now, the food-trolley was beside me.

'Excuse me, sir! What would you like to have for lunch?' the air hostess asked.

'You are excused, baby,' I thought, forcing myself to change my mood. Aloud, I said, 'Hmm . . . A sandwich with a Coke will do.'

'You don't want to have lunch?' She was surprised.

'This is my lunch for today.'

'Ok. Veg or non-veg, sir?' She smiled.

Wow! This time that smile appeared good to me.

'You won't be serving me both?' I asked her as soon as she completed her question.

She looked at the food on her trolley, a little flustered, probably counting to see if she could spare two.

'Hey, I was kidding. Give me a veg sandwich,' I said, interrupting her.

She again smiled and served me the sandwich and Coke. I forced myself to come out of that gloomy mood.

'Wow! That smile is pretty indeed,' I told myself. The next moment I had this weird urge to check out her name tag. I don't know why, but I felt that she was a Punjabi too. But before I could do that, she had gone to the row behind me. I tried to stand up a bit and turned back to look, but then I noticed that the fat lady beside me was staring at me, as if she had caught a guy in her neighborhood making passes at her daughter.

('You Men are dogs,' Khushi always used to say to me. 'And you are going to marry one of them, no?' was my reply every time.) I sat back on my seat with a little disappointment and had my sandwich and coke.

I only realized I had fallen asleep when the announcement woke me up: 'Ladies and gentlemen, we are about to land at Delhi airport in a short while.'

I became very anxious again, recalling the purpose for which I was traveling. A little later, I would be seeing Khushi in the ICU. I raised the window's shutter to have a look at the view outside. It was drizzling.

All of a sudden, I felt a bit cold. Not due to the weather, but because of my nervousness and anxiety about her condition.

At 1.45, forty-five minutes late due to bad weather, the plane landed. In fifteen minutes, I managed to collect my air-bag and was outside the airport. At a distance, amid the crowd in front of me, I saw Deepu and Jiju waving to me. I waved back and moved towards them. Meanwhile, I switched on my mobile and saw some missed calls from Deepu.

'How are you?' Deepu asked, shaking my hand.

'I am fine. How are you and any update on Khushi's present condition?' I asked, with my fingers crossed.

He then gave me an update, with some medical terms that were new to me. But, somehow, they did not make me feel good. I then asked him if the overall situation was better than yesterday.

'Hmm . . .' Deepu was trying to frame his next sentence. I understood the situation.

I then acknowledged Jiju's presence. This was the first time I was seeing him.

'This is our elder Jiju,' Deepu introduced me.

'*Sat Sri Akal*,' I said and shook his hand.

'I believe the flight got late,' he said.

'Yes, because of this weather . . . they wanted us to enjoy the scenic beauty of Delhi from up there,' I pointed towards the sky with a smile, trying to make everyone a little relaxed.

We got into a cab. Delhi was quite chilly and I wanted to feel the cold so I took off my jacket. It took us more than an hour to reach the hospital in Faridabad. The cab driver left us at the entrance and drove to the parking lot.

We went into the hospital and took the elevator to the second floor. As I was getting closer to her, my fear was increasing and I started shaking a bit. I looked at the different faces in the elevator and their expressions which told their happy and sad stories. On the second floor, the elevator door opened.

Stepping out, I saw Pushkar coming towards me. I hugged him. Before he could ask anything about my journey and me, I asked him about her condition.

'The doctors have updated me about her condition a few minutes back,' Pushkar said, looking at all of us.

'What kind of update. Tell me?' I asked.

'She is still unconscious but her condition is a little better since morning, though she is not yet completely out of danger. They are planning to operate on her fractured jaw and thighs in a day or two. Apart from that there are some blood clots in some section of her brain, though they're not that critical and are likely to heal through medication.'

That 'little better' made us all feel a little better. Still, we were worried.

Though we knew that Pushkar has told us everything the doctors had told him, we kept asking him more questions, hoping that at least *something* would be positive.

Meanwhile, there was an announcement on that floor for all of us who were without ICU passes to go to the ground floor as the meeting time was over. Every evening, between 5.30 and 6, one or two people from the patients' families were allowed to visit. I looked back to see where this announcement came from.

There I saw a door with the letters 'I C U' engraved on it. Intensive Care Unit. The meaning of the acronym made me shiver. A raw fear passed through me. This was the first time in my life I was standing in front of an ICU door, thinking about the person on the other side and what she meant to me and my life.

'God, please,' I said, staring at those bold letters.

I tried to look in from the little glass window embedded in that door.

'The path on the right side leads to her bed. Bed number 3,' a person standing behind me said.

I looked back.

'This is Susant,' Deepu said and introduced us.

'Oh yes, Khushi used to talk about you.'

Khushi and Susant were in the same college and he used to treat her like his own sister.

Amid our introductions, there was a second announcement bidding us to vacate the ICU floor. It was decided that Susant would stay back in the hospital that evening and we all would go home. At night, one of us would come back to replace Susant.

At 6.15 p.m., we reached home. The door was open and I was the first person to enter, carrying my airbag on my shoulder. While entering the drawing room I saw Khushi's mum. She seemed to be very worried—a mother whose child was fighting the most crucial battle of her life. Keeping my bag on the ground, I went to her to touch her feet and she hugged me like her own son.

I whispered in her ears, 'Everything will be fine, absolutely fine.'

'Yes. Now that you have come, she will be fine,' she said patting my back with affection.

Meanwhile, I saw Misha di and Ami di. I met them, answering their questions about my hassle-free journey. We sat on the sofas and chairs in the drawing room. A little later, her dad came in from the other room. I got up to touch his feet and he, too, inquired if my journey had been fine.

We then sat discussing whatever had happened during the last two days. He was describing the probable conditions in which the accident had taken place. Amid our discussions, there were moments of long silences and deep breaths which we all were trying to break with our positive words.

I then saw Neeru coming out of the kitchen with some water and tea on a tray. 'Look at her face and the grief which has replaced her sweet smile,' I thought to myself. She came and placed the cups on the table in front of us. She was about to leave without talking to me, when I said, 'Hi, Neeru.'

'Hello. How are you?'

'I am fine. And how about you?'

'I am fine too,' she said, picking up the used glasses and silently returning to the kitchen.

'She's terribly sad,' Mumma said to me.

'I can understand.'

We continued talking for a little while, after which everyone got busy with their respective tasks. I then saw little Daan running out of the other room with his toys. He recognized me immediately and, coming to me, he asked, 'You've come again?'

'Yes. I have come to see you, dear,' I answered, taking him in my arms.

'What have you got for me?' I was expecting this question.

'Well, I have chocolates for you sweetheart! But you will get them if you give me ten kisses,' I said, gently pressing his sweet cheeks.

He did not say anything, but started kissing me and counting, after which I handed him his chocolates. He was so happy that he rushed to his mother to show her.

'Never forget to get chocolates for Daan,' was Khushi's sweet command for me. She kept reminding me of such sweet and caring tasks which had so much importance in her life.

We had our dinner at 9 that night, after which we were discussing who would be the two persons going to stay in the hospital for the night. Every male member in the family was willing to be there and I counted myself part of this family too.

'You might be tired after your journey. So better you rest here at home,' Dad said to me.

'No, I'm fine. My journey was hardly three hours . . .'

I badly wanted to go to the hospital. I wanted to be as close as possible to her. But then, a little later, Dad finally decided that Deepu and Jiju would go to the hospital and I should remain at home that night. Pushkar had to go to his office to complete some work.

I was disappointed. I badly wanted to see her. But now, I had to spend another sleepless night without seeing her.

At 11.30 I was in bed, in Khushi's room. Alone, I was looking here and there at the things in her room and trying to recollect what she used to tell me about them during our conversations. The computer on my right, her closet on the left and the store-room, attached to this room, full of books. The disappointment of not being able to make it to the hospital that night was reduced a little by the thought that I was going to spend that night in her room, on the bed where she used to sleep.

With all these thoughts in mind, I don't remember when I fell asleep. I must have slept for a few hours. The next time I woke up, there was a little noise coming out of the attached bathroom. The lights in the room had been switched off and there was a blanket covering me from shoulder to toe. I checked my cell to see the time. It was 5 a.m. Somebody then switched on the light in the bathroom. I tried to figure out what that sound was. Soon, I realized that it was the tap water falling in the empty, giant tub in the bathroom.

'Ah! She used to tell me this,' I thought with a little excitement. Khushi used to tell me about this irritating thing in most of our 'good morning' calls.

Completely awake now, I smiled, remembering her narration. How well she had described this moment, which was so painful for a person who wanted to sleep. And just like she had told me, her mother came out of the bathroom and turned the green night lamp on before leaving the room. I felt as if I had won some championship for knowing, in advance, what would happen. How well I knew my Khushi, I thought. We were made for each other . . .

I covered my face with the blanket, trying to escape that greenish light and the sound of water falling in the tub.

'Jesus! How does she bear this every morning?' I wondered and went back to sleep.

The next morning, I woke up around eight and saw Mumma in the other room, trying to wake her daughters up every ten minutes.

I went up to her and said, 'Good morning, Mumma.'

'Good morning, *beta ji*,' she replied, 'Look at them, they are so lazy.' She pointed at them, with a little frustration and a smile at the same time.

I looked at where she was pointing and saw Ami di and Misha di fighting for the common blanket in their sleep. I felt pity for the poor blanket which was being pulled here and there so often. The heads and feet, coming out of the blanket at odd angles, posed questions about their sleeping posture which were hard to answer, at least for me. Amid this fight for the blanket, Neeru was very calm in her sleep. Nothing was bothering her, not even her mother's wake-up calls. Watching them with a smile, I was about to go to the bathroom when I saw a little hand coming out of Neeru's long hair.

'Hey! Who's that?' I said in a sweet voice, trying to uncover little Daan who was sandwiched in between his *maasis*. He looked so very sweet in his sleep that I could not resist giving him a good morning kiss. The four of them sleeping on that bed appeared so good to me. Looking at them, I realized how much they loved each other and how close-knit this family was.

'Touchwood,' I said in my heart.

I was amazed at the morning in this house being so good. And when Khushi would be back here, it will be simply awesome. I wished I could soon see all the siblings in this house, sleeping in their funny way.

By 9.20 I was ready and through with my morning prayers. While coming out of my room I saw Neeru and Ami di in the kitchen. I wanted to crack a little joke then, recalling the morning's sight. But I checked myself, maybe because of the thoughts of Khushi's condition running in everyone's mind and mine, or the silence that pervaded the home. And if not that either, then because of Dad's serious presence at the dining table.

'We are getting late for the hospital. Why is the breakfast not ready yet?' Dad asked the females of the house, looking at the kitchen door.

We had to reach the hospital and send Jiju and Deepu, who had been there all night, back home.

No one but Mumma dared to answer the question. 'It's almost done,' she said.

And in a short while, breakfast was served. Dad called me to join him and, of course, I did accordingly. We took nearly twenty minutes to have our breakfast and at ten, we left for the hospital. On our way, suddenly, I had the same feeling that I had the day before when, for the first time, I was entering the ICU, wishing to see her.

Soon, we were in the hospital. On the ICU floor, I saw Deepu half-asleep in a corner chair in the hall. Dad and I went straight to him.

'Hey Deepu,' I said, placing my hand on his shoulder.

He woke up with a start and looked up. He was tired and I could see the sleep in his eyes.

'Hi,' he said, getting up from his seat.

'Did the doctors see her this morning?' Dad asked him.

'Yes, they saw her. In fact, a little while ago, they talked to me and said that they will be going for a CT scan by noon. They want to check the present status of the blood clots in didi's brain.'

Meanwhile, Jiju joined our conversation. He had gone to get a water bottle from the shop in the hospital campus. He too got an update from Deepu. A little later, Dad asked both of them to go back home so that they could have breakfast and take some rest. But Jiju insisted on staying there for a while, with us. He suspected that the doctors might be taking Khushi for the CT scan soon and then he too could see her. So he stayed back, while Deepu left for home in his car. Deepu was definitely not going to rest, as there was important work at home to be completed.

The three of us occupied vacant chairs in different rows on that floor. I started looking at the people around me—some sleeping, some talking to their dear ones on their mobiles, some chanting prayers and a few wiping their tears. Deep in their eyes was a fear which they were fighting against. There was this smell in the air, peculiar to every hospital in this country. In front of us was the ICU door which was scaring me an awful lot.

In the right corner of this floor there was a TV set, at a height. Some India versus Sri Lanka series was on, with the volume almost zero. A few youngsters were following the match before a lady demanded to see the repeat telecast of a *Saas-Bahu* serial which she had missed last night. According to the person sitting next to me, this lady was quite happy today as her father-in-law was being discharged from the ICU in a few hours. The moment she heard this news from her doctor, she discovered a way to celebrate by watching reruns of her favorite soap.

So much was happening around me. Every five minutes, the elevator door opened in order to flush out and take in different people. Nurses and ward boys wheeled patients on trolleys to different rooms on the other side of the ICU door. Frequent announcements called for attendants to meet their respective doctors and, with every call, the concerned persons rushed to the ICU in hope and fear.

This was an altogether new atmosphere for me or, probably, for everyone on this floor. The doctors on the other side of the ICU door seemed like Gods to us and the gatekeeper at the entrance, their messenger. And just like a temple, we were supposed to remove our shoes at the door before moving in. At times, the same door opened from the other side and we saw people coming out, some smiling, some about to burst into tears.

Finally, there was an announcement for us too. 'Bed no. 3. Attendants of Khushi, please come in.'

This was enough to send my heart racing. Despite the sweat on my forehead, all of a sudden I felt extremely cold inside. I started breathing heavily. I knew the time had come when I was going to see something which would disturb me. I looked at Dad and Jiju and then the three of us rushed towards the door. By now, none of us had seen her and I don't know what was happening to them, but I was shaking. I felt Jiju's hand on my shoulder trying to comfort me as we approached the door.

'Yes,' Dad said to the gatekeeper.

'Go to the CT scan room on the ground floor. The nurses have taken her there for the scan,' the gatekeeper told us.

We rushed towards the elevator. The door was about to close when we squeezed ourselves in. At the ground floor, outside the elevator door, I asked the guard for directions to the CT-scan room. Busy with his cellphone he pointed the way. I was running, with Dad and Jiju trying to catch up. I passed by many rooms on this floor and finally reached the zone where I saw a board which read 'CT scan'. The entrance to this zone was a grill-like structure behind which there was a reception counter.

'Yes?' one of the ladies at the reception asked me.

'Has the CT scan of the patient named Khushi started?' I asked her, tying my shoelace which had come undone while I was running.

She glanced at the last entries in her thick register. Meanwhile, I turned back to see Dad and Jiju, who were still four blocks away from this room.

'Can you see that stretcher inside, behind that green curtain? That's your patient and the CT scan is about to start in a short while,' she said, pointing towards the CT-scan room.

'Who are you and . . .' she tried to ask me but, before she could complete her questions, my feet started moving towards that stretcher. All of a sudden I was calm. I felt everything around me was freezing, as if time was slowing down every second. The voices around me grew dim in my ears. I was seeing people around me and their actions but was not able to hear them at all. I could see the reception lady behind me still asking so many questions and prohibiting me from going in, but I was not able to understand her and I kept walking towards the green curtain without even blinking. At the door, the ward boy tried to stop me, possibly at the receptionist's command. I don't remember his face and what had happened to him, but there was something, something because of which he took his hands off me the very next moment. Maybe it was my tears falling on his hands . . .

And, finally, I was standing beside her.

Seeing her, my heart melted inside me. Never in my worst nightmare could I have seen her this way. My sweetheart, my Khushi was in front of me and her body revealed what she had gone through. Most of her body was covered with a white bed sheet. Her innocent face had suffered so many injuries. There were blood clots on her swollen right eye. There were scars, big and small, on her entire face. A thick ventilator tube ran down her nose. Her broken jaw was temporarily fixed with bandages. The soft skin of her right arm bore the marks of so many injections that it had turned blue. I could see multiple tubes of different diameters piercing different parts of her body. On her bed she was surrounded by various medical equipment including a ventilator, a small monitor to read the heart-beat, an oxygen-cylinder extension and medicine bags with injections and medicine in them. And there were these constant beeps from the ventilator.

I saw her hand, coming out from under the bed sheet at my side. I touched her little finger very gently. In response, I felt her beautiful fingers crawling on my palm and, with that, I suddenly held her hand and started crying, seeing my dearest bearing that pain all alone.

I felt a hand on my shoulder again. Regaining my senses, I looked back to see Jiju standing behind me looking at her. Dad approached her from the other side and was observing her with love and warmth in his eyes. Indeed, it's hard for a father to see his daughter breathing with the help of a support system. And there I was, still holding her hand. The three of us, standing beside our dear Khushi, were praying hard, with all our heart and soul.

'We have to take her for the scan,' a feminine voice broke the silence in that room. She was the nurse who was in charge and had been to get the CT scan machine ready.

She called the ward boy at the entrance for help and wheeled the stretcher to the scanner. It was a giant, white-coloured, wheel-like structure which I had seen earlier only in some movies. I was feeling apprehensive.

'Help me to shift her to the scanner,' the nurse said in a loud voice while assembling the ventilator tube.

We all helped in shifting her from the stretcher. I was standing on her left along with the nurse. Dad and Jiju were at the other side. The ward boy too came and stood beside us in order to lift her. We all were at our positions, but I couldn't understand how we would shift her with all the equipment and various tubes attached to her badly injured body.

'Now,' the nurse said, commanding all of us to lift her.

All hands were at work that moment. Though Dad, Jiju and I took utmost care in transferring her to the scanner, the nurse did not seem careful enough to me. She lifted her from the stretcher without giving any support to her neck and, moreover, the way she gripped her hand was definitely not right.

'The saline tube has come out,' the ward boy said.

I jumped and caught hold of that tube to give it to the nurse as soon as possible so that she could fix it. But the nurse appeared too lazy to do that.

'Please fix that thing first,' I said to her.

'Relax, sir. Everyday we handle many patients. Don't worry,' she said, arrogantly.

'Yes, and that's why you have become so callous,' I said silently.

Khushi had started showing some movement in her hands, which was gradually increasing, maybe because of the pain. In a little while, she was literally shaking her hands to get rid of the needles piercing her hand. Seeing her, I panicked and asked the nurse to do something.

'She is in a sub-conscious state where everybody reacts this way. Nothing new,' she answered, completely ignoring my panic.

Maybe not for her, but it was definitely new for me. I was not able to stand seeing my better-half in that state. I was getting frustrated by the nurse's behavior but I knew we were not in a position to do anything which might add to our miseries. I stood beside Khushi, holding her hands in mine in order to prevent her from taking off the saline and ventilator tubes.

'Apart from you, everybody can leave this room,' the nurse said pointing at me.

'Why?' I asked her in a gentle tone.

'We are going to begin the scan and usually we allow attendants to stay only if we need them. I need you to hold her hands throughout the scan or she might take off her saline needle,' she explained.

Dad, Jiju and the ward boy left the room. The nurse closed the door from inside and gave me a sleeveless jacket, to protect me from the rays coming out of that giant white wheel, I think. She then went inside the control room to operate the machine. Back in this room, I was standing, holding my beloved's hands, looking at her face. My heart bargaining with God, 'Anything, but not her.'

Gradually I felt the strength with which she was trying to shake her hands. It was getting difficult for me to hold her firmly without hurting her. No one was around us. I steeled myself to hold her tight.

And I started talking to her.

'Hey, dear. I am so sorry if I am hurting you, but this is for your good. I am doing this because I want you to get well soon. I am doing this because you are the best thing that ever happened to me and I don't want to see that going away from me because I simply cannot think of living without you. Come back to me, please. Open your eyes and see, your Shona is here for you.'

Holding her hands in mine, I bent down to whisper in her ears, 'Fight. Fight for me. For all of us. And I promise you, we will provide you the best hospital, the best doctors, the best medicine and the best care.'

For rest of the few minutes, I kept seeing her face.

Meanwhile, the nurse came in from the control room confirming that the scan was done. I realized that the sound coming from the machine wasn't there any more. She opened the door and I saw Dad and Jiju standing outside, looking at me.

With the help of the ward boy, we then shifted her back to the stretcher. This time, I took care to shift the saline pouch, the urine bag and the ventilator along with her. I didn't want anybody to make any mistake this time. After shifting her back to the stretcher, the ward boy wheeled her out of the scan room. We too were walking along with them. Back at the entrance, I saw the reception lady again, looking at me. 'I am sorry,' I said and passed by her. On the way back to the ICU the nurse took a different route—an elevator that led to the ICU. Our entrance was prohibited. We stood there, seeing them taking her away.

I joined my palms, praying to God to take care of her and make her get well soon. Then we returned to the ICU attendant-hall, back on the same chairs, amid the same crowd, hearing similar announcements. A little later, Jiju left for home after Dad insisted that he go and take some rest. Dad and I spent the rest of the time in the hospital sitting on our chair, confined to the attendant-hall.

Whatever I had seen in the past few hours was flashing through my brain. Her face, her hands and my one-sided conversation with her.

'Did she recognize my voice? Did she hear me talking to her? Did she want to say something to me?' These were the questions I was asking myself again and again. For hours, I struggled with these questions and bad thoughts at one end, and prayers and hopes at the other.

It was 3 p.m. when Pushkar arrived at the hospital with a lunch-box. I met him while I was coming out of the restroom and updated him about today's CT scan.

'So did the doctors talk about the reports too?' he asked.

'Not yet. They might, during the evening counseling hours,' I said.

'Hmm . . . I thought so. By the way, I have got lunch for you and Dad and me,' he said.

'I think it would be better to send Dad back home, so that he can have his lunch comfortably there and rest a little. He seems to be tired.'

'That's fine. I'll be here with you.'

We then moved towards the attendant-hall.

Despite Dad's reluctance, we succeeded in sending him back home.

I had my lunch after that. For the next few hours, Pushkar and I were talking to each other, about our office, family and friends. And our Khushi.

It was 5.30 in the evening when we saw Deepu coming out of the elevator. The visiting hours had started and I knew he was here to see his sister. He sat beside us, talking about the little problem with his car and that it needed servicing. Dad had already told him about the morning's CT scan.

When our turn was announced, we asked him to go ahead to the ICU. Back in the hall, Pushkar and I were worried about the

CT-scan report. Our eyes were glued to the ICU door, waiting for Deepu to come out with some update from the doctors. And nearly fifteen minutes later, we saw him coming out. We got up from our seats and went to him.

'The doctors say that the blood clots are still persisting in didi's brain. But the good thing is that they have not worsened,' he said before we could ask him.

'Anything else?' I wanted to know.

'Nothing as such. She is in a subconscious state and moving her hands and legs.'

We stood near that ICU door for a while before we walked back to our seats, where we sat for another hour or so. Meanwhile, Dad called up Deepu on his cell. He wanted me to come back home. Though I was not willing to leave the hospital, the frequent announcements finally made me leave. According to the announcements, only the attendants having ICU passes were allowed to stay back on this floor and the checking was about to begin. We just had two passes with us and one of us had to leave. I did not feel like asking either Pushkar or Deepu to do so and so I agreed to go.

'I'll drop you home,' Deepu said.

'OK,' I said looking at him and Pushkar.

'Have some tea at home and relax a bit. You've been here since morning,' Pushkar said, patting my shoulder.

'I will. See you later.'

'See you.'

While going down in the elevator, I was asking myself—and God, if He could answer me—when she was going to open her eyes and talk to me. When would I hear the doctors say that she is out of danger? When will things be all right for all of us again? I begged God to talk to me and answer my questions.

Once at the ground floor, we came out of the hospital. It was cold outside. Deepu was saying something to me which I ignored, stuck in my one-sided conversation with God. Looking down at the road, lost in my thoughts, I walked out of the hospital exit following Deepu's footsteps.

'That's our car, over there,' Deepu pointed.

Without responding, I followed him and got in the car. My silence was obtrusive. But then something happened in that car which made me feel good and broke my silence. The moment he started the engine, the music system turned on and the paused song continued:

'I am gonna wake up . . . It's not my time to go . . . I guess I will die another day . . .'

I heard the words very clearly, coming out of the music system in his car that night. Making myself comfortable on the seat now, I was wondering if this was just another song or if it was God himself trying to make my conversation two-sided, or if this was Khushi somehow conveying what she wanted to tell me when I was holding her hands in mine. I don't know what it was but, those lyrics were more than just words. Or maybe it is human tendency to choose something which gives the maximum comfort.

'Amen,' I wished in my heart and, feeling a little better, started talking to Deepu.

We reached home and after a while Deepu was about to leave when Dad asked him to have dinner first, so that he didn't have to come back again. In the living room I saw Jiju and Daan playing with each other. Seeing me, Neeru prepared some tea for both Jiju and me. For the next half an hour, the entire family was in the living-room. That night, we had our dinner at around nine, after which Deepu left for the hospital. I wanted to go back to the hospital with him, but I knew Susant was going to accompany him there for the night. Moreover, someone at home mentioned that Susant would be traveling to Chandigarh tomorrow and would return after two or three days. I thought

I'd replace him on those successive nights. Pushkar was supposed to leave for his office that night for some important calls.

I spent that night in her room again, on her bed. Before closing my eyes I recollected moments from our happy days and prayed to God to heal her. And so another day in my life passed in prayers, hope and anxiety.

The next day was pretty much like the previous one. Dad, Jiju and I were at the hospital by 10.30 a.m. Deepu told us about the doctors' plan to operate on her thighs and jaw that very day. According to them, she was in a better condition now and thus they were going ahead with the surgery. We were asked to replace a jaw-plate at the hospital bank, as the doctors were going to use one while operating on her jaw. Moreover, we had to arrange four blood donors for replacement as approximately four units of blood was going to be used for the operation.

I didn't know about this blood-replacement principle earlier. Dad told me that whenever a blood unit is used for a patient, the same amount has to be replaced by the attendants of the patient, usually within twenty-four hours. It was not about getting some certified blood from a blood bank—what we needed was people who would donate their blood in this hospital's blood donation center.

'So we are now supposed to search four donors whose blood groups are A+ and are willing to give us blood in the next twenty-four hours?' I asked Dad. I knew that, in her entire family, only her Dad was A+ and everyone else was O+, even me.

'No, for replacement, donors can be of any blood group. The only condition is that an equivalent number of units needs to be donated. And we already have arranged the donors,' Deepu clarified.

'Who are they?' I asked

'Two of Susant's close friends, the admin from CSC and me.'

'Even I can be a donor. We can ask one of Susant's friends to stay back,' I said.

'Everybody is here by now and we should judiciously use persons from our family to donate blood. There can be worst-case scenarios any moment, where we might not find others to donate blood on time. Remember, if you donate blood now, you can't for the next three months.' He had a point. I just wished that the worst-case scenarios would not arrive.

'I will go with Susant's friends to the blood bank and after that I will leave for home. Need to have some food before donating blood,' he said and went off.

My cellphone rang, then. I looked at my watch while taking the cell from my pocket. It was 11 and I knew this was mom's call. She would ring me twice everyday to get an update about our discussions with the doctors.

'*Sat Sri Akal*, Mumma,' I said, moving out of the crowded hall.

'*Sat Sri Akal, beta*. How are you?'

'I am fine. How is your backache? Any relief?'

'It's the same as before. It becomes troublesome at times, but I am fine. Any update on Khushi's condition?'

I told her about the doctor's decision to operate on Khushi today and the blood replenishment thing. She expressed concern about the operation and I tried to comfort her, saying it was because Khushi was better today that the doctors could take this decision. As usual, she also asked me about Khushi's mother and rest of the family. Before hanging up, she consoled me, as always, saying that God is great and would take care of her.

'Yeah, I know she will be fine. You take care and I will call you again in the evening.' With that, I hung up and moved back to the attendant-hall to locate Dad and Jiju.

'They are going to start the operation at 1.30,' Dad told me.

'Do we need to do anything else for the operation, apart from the donors and the jaw-plate replacement?' I asked.

'I asked but, according to the doctors, we don't need to do anything else at our end.'

The operation began on time, that afternoon. I was told that it was going to take at least three hours. We all were now sitting in a different waiting-hall on the 1st floor of the building. In front was a door with 'OT' written on it and a red bulb above it which was switched on.

The anxiety and the chill were back in me and I think it was the same with all of us. We were scarcely talking. Stranded between fear and hope, pacing up and down the waiting-hall. Time stood still. Minutes passed like hours, hours like days. And all along, there were our fears and hopes, battling with each other, winning and losing at different moments.

I stood at the window, watching the traffic outside and the weather which was changing drastically. All of a sudden it was getting dark. Black clouds hovered in the skies of Faridabad. It was going to rain heavily. I was still looking through the window when my phone rang. It was Happy. I picked up his call.

'Hey! Happy *veer*.'

'Hey! How is my brother doing and how is my bhabhi now?'

'They are operating on the fractures in her thighs and jaw. It's going to take two more hours.'

'But when I last called, you said the doctors were not going to operate on her so soon?'

'Yes, but this morning they said that she was in a better condition to be operated now.'

'That means she is improving.'

'I hope so. I just want to see her well *yaar*,' I said in a low voice.

'Oh, come on, buddy. She is going to be absolutely fine. See, she has shown some improvement, that's why the doctors have gone ahead with the operation. It's just a matter of time and we will be dancing together to the beats of *bhangra* at your engagement . . . What say?' He tried to console me and make me feel better.

'Yeah,' I said. 'I just need her so badly . . . every damn thought is shaking me inside and . . . You know how madly I love her. I feel so lonely in this crowd just because I am not able to talk to her.'

'I know dear. But take this as a challenge, as a test, and I am sure you will come out of it with flying colours. Just think of the good time which is going to come after this hard time, when she will open her eyes and talk to you.'

I wished every single letter of what he said would come true, no matter what. I was about to ask him something when, all of a sudden, I started losing his voice. I could see water splashing on the window, a few inches from my nose. In no time, it had started raining heavily and all I could say was, 'I can't hear you . . . It's raining heavily,' before the phone got disconnected.

I looked out of the window to see people rushing into the hospital or their vehicles. Seeing that rain, all of a sudden I had this unbearable urge to hear her voice. She used to enjoy the rains while talking to me and, maybe because of that, I too had developed a romantic tendency to talk to her when it rained. It was a long time since I had last heard her voice and I badly wanted to hear my beloved voice again.

I ran outside in that heavy rain. I searched for a cyber café and satisfied my urge by listening to the voice messages she left for me while I was abroad.

I was completely drenched from outside.

And from inside.

~

One evening, just like any weekday evening, I am playing snooker with my friends at my office's health club.

Khushi is giving me missed calls, wanting me to call her. The balance in her cellphone is low. But I am not calling her back. I am busy playing my game. In a couple of months there is a Snooker tournament in Infosys, Bhubaneswar, and I am practicing hard for it.

My phone rings for the third time. I disconnect.

She calls again. I am pissed off and pick up the call.

'What?'

'Why aren't you picking up the phone?'

'I am practicing snooker. You know that I am busy playing at this time.'

'You don't have time for me? Not even five minutes?'

'Khushi, please! Can we talk later? They all are waiting for my shot.'

'Ok, bye.'

I keep my cellphone far away from the snooker table and resume playing. An hour later, after winning the rack of the last game, I go back to pick my phone.

> *There is a message in it. From her.*
> *U might be happy 2 win d tournament,*
> *bt someday u might b sad, wen u might*
> *wish 2 tlk 2 me bt I might not b able 2 do so.*

~

Nothing changed. Even after four days, things remained the same—her unconsciousness, the doctors' inability to say anything definite, our fears, our prayers and our tears.

Time and again, we were asking the doctors if we needed to take any second opinion on her treatment. If we could get her treated somewhere else before it was too late. But they were non-committal.

With each passing day, her battle with death was getting more difficult. Constantly being on the ventilator, she got pneumonia, her lungs were lacking blood. She started bleeding somewhere inside her intestine. She had already been given ten units of blood but her falling blood pressure didn't gain any sustenance.

The threat of the worst changed me. All of a sudden, I started believing in all kinds of superstitions and myths. Had anyone told me—'Pick up a few pebbles from the road and eat them. It will save her.'—I would have done that too. I was so desperate to make her well that I was ready to do anything. Anything. Without a second thought.

The mental burden I was carrying—we all were carrying—was just too much. Waiting, hoping for some good news, which we did not get. Instead, the bad news, the new miseries kept piling on. I could even feel my helplessness and frustration leading to a mental breakdown. And it was hard to stay positive and not lose my cool and patience.

Later that evening, the doctors permitted us to take a second opinion for her treatment. Which meant that they felt they could not do more. Her condition was deteriorating.

We all made up our mind. Apollo Hospital was our last medical hope.

Moving a patient who was so serious was going to be the toughest part of her treatment. Taking her out from the atmosphere of a protected ICU into the open air full of bacteria and viruses, then her transit from Faridabad to Delhi in an ambulance, running amid the busiest traffic—all this involved so much risk. Even the thought of it gave me jitters. A single mistake could lead to disaster. But we had no other alternative.

The next day, we all were geared up for the big task. I remember well, it was *Mahavir Jayanti* and, in my heart, I had this feeling that we all were going to do well on that auspicious day.

But fate kept threatening us time and again. We were about to take her out of the hospital when her dad was asked to do something. We were given a set of documents to be signed and the last one was a disclaimer which read:

'The patient's condition is serious and this entire transition is being done on the wish of patient's family. In case of any further damage which may/may not lead to the death of the patient, the hospital will not be held responsible.'

Her father signed that paper and we came out after making the entire payment.

In the next half an hour, we were on the road. Every single minute involved extreme caution. Throughout, I kept saying God's name in my heart. It was the first time I had been in an ambulance. Being in an ambulance is so different from being on the road, watching an ambulance. I never knew it was so frightening. The siren kept torturing me. Everything was going fine, still, every now and then, I kept asking the doctor with us. And, every time, his response was positive.

Passing those forty-five minutes of restlessness, we finally reached Apollo. They immediately took her to the ICU and we were asked to complete the formalities. It took us almost an hour after which we were allowed to see her just once. I was the last person to leave the ICU. I stood there in front of a new doctor who was going to handle her case. He was the senior-most person amid all those people in white aprons and his team got busy studying the MRI and X-Rays. I wanted to talk to him. But when he appeared in front of me, waiting for me to say something, I just could not.

'What happened?' he asked, placing his hand on my shoulder.

'A . . .'

'Yes?'

I looked down, trying to speak.

'Son! What happened?' He raised my chin.

'Can you save her for me?' was all I could say before tears ran down my face.

'That's what we always try to do here. Don't worry, things will get better. You take care of yourself. We will take care of her.'

Somebody called him and he got busy again, studying her reports.

I came out of the ICU. The toughest job of the day was over. She was successfully admitted in her new hospital. There was a feeling of victory and a new ray of hope within our hearts.

Later that night, talking to her mom, Dad said, 'She is now in safer hands.'

That was the first night since her accident when I slept a little better.

'But you said she was going to be all right!'

'See, gentlemen, don't lose your calm. We can't promise you the moon. We are trying our best.'

The next evening, I was talking to the doctors. They were saying that her condition was deteriorating because of the fall in her platelet count. Suddenly, things appeared very different from what we had planned, what we had hoped and expected.

Later, in the middle of the night, an alarm-bell rang when the doctors told us, 'Her body needs blood.'

'Blood? Again?' I asked.

'This time, we need platelets to be injected into her body. Their level has fallen way below the expected.'

'We can get that from the blood bank, right?' her dad asked.

'These cells don't last for more than four to six hours. So they can't be stored in a blood bank. We need people who can donate plasma cells to her.'

'So can I donate those cells?' I asked. 'Only a person whose blood group matches hers and whose cell-match test is positive can donate.'

'How much time do we have?'

'We need to do this as soon as possible,' they replied and returned to work, in haste.

The situation was really bad. Apart from her dad, no one else in her entire family had the A+ blood group. And worse, he was prohibited from donating blood because of his old age. In the middle of that tough night, Deepu, Dad and I were facing another challenge.

Deepu was trying to get in touch with all possible contacts. We also gave a call to the HR folks in her office to see if there was any possibility to get a blood-match from her co-workers. I dialed Pushkar's number to tell him about the need of the moment.

Half an hour later, we got to hear something positive. Some guy from his office, whose blood group matched with hers, was ready. But our bad luck didn't let up. He had consumed liquor that evening in a party. There was alcohol in his blood and the test report said, 'Negative.'

An hour later, Deepu managed to get some good news. Someone in their neighborhood had agreed to help. As soon as that person appeared, he was taken to the lab for the initial tests. In a while, we learnt that his blood matched the requirements and he went to donate his platelets. Back in the waiting-room, we felt a little relaxed knowing that we were able to meet the immediate needs.

After his blood donation, I was talking to the person who was no less than God's own messenger.

'I don't know you and I don't know how to thank you,' I said.

'If not me, then someone else,' he replied, sipping fruit juice served by the hospital staff.

We arranged a cab to drop him back home.

'She is a nice person. I know her. Don't worry; she will be fine soon,' he said as he sat in the cab and shook hands with me. I didn't know what to say to that person. Words were not enough for the help he had given us.

At around three in the morning, Deepu's cousin brother reached the hospital. It was his turn to stay back and we all left for home to take some rest.

But the fear that something worse would come up again still persisted deep inside me.

Her condition showed a little improvement in the next ten hours. The plasma count in her blood was better than before. But she was not in a stage where the doctors could say that she was out of danger. They could not be sure of a positive development, but they gave us hope.

Back in my hometown, my family was worried about me. It was a week since I had left them. First, my Mumma was concerned about Khushi, and then for me. She was worried about all that must be going on in my mind amid all this. She knew I was not doing well. Mumma wanted to be with me at this time. She could make out that I needed her. She too wanted to be with me. My father said she had not been feeling well for the last two days. She wanted to see Khushi, the girl she had been talking to for months.

When I called her up, she asked me if I could come back to her and then, both of us could return to Faridabad. I had no idea what I should do, though I wanted her to be with me.

Then, something else came to my attention, as I was living with her family. The people visiting her home were making me self-conscious. When her family was questioned about my identity. When they were asked, 'So he is staying with you? Since a week?' Such questions made me apprehensive. Was I making their life uncomfortable? People at times talk shit, I knew that. I was not bothered about myself, but I didn't want to be the source of trouble and gossip about their family.

In next twenty-four hours, a few more units of blood platelets were given to her. We managed to get the support of everyone in her office. Their HR asked for donations through mails from the employees.

Soon things seemed to be getting better. Our endless efforts were showing results. Her blood platelet count was returning to normal.

Later that evening, Khushi's dad told me that my mom had called him up. He said that my family needed me.

'Your mom was so worried. She wants to see you and she wishes to be here. If you wish, you can go back and bring her with you.'

'I understand her situation. But I don't want to leave Khushi in this condition.'

'We all are here to take care of her. Let's think wisely and handle things well. I will leave the decision to you.'

'I will talk to the doctors and then make my decision.'

I went to the doctor's chamber. There was a lady doctor whom I had sometimes seen diagnosing Khushi. She was part of the team handling her case.

'Ma'am, can I talk to you for a while?'

'Yes.' And before I could walk up to her desk, she asked, 'You are from the family of the patient on bed number 305, right?'

'Uh . . . Yes, Ma'am.'

'Tell me.'

'Ma'am, due to certain reasons my family wants me back for a short time. My mom needs me and I have to bring her here along with me. As I'm not mentally prepared to do this, I want your suggestion.' I was silent for a moment, then added, 'You understand what I mean?'

'I do,' she said and asked me, 'May I know your relation to the patient?'

'She is my fiancée.'

'Oh, I thought you were family.'

'By now, I am a member of her family,' I said very clearly.

She looked at me for a while and then looked at my hands.

'Just two days before our engagement, she met with this accident.

It's just the ring that's left, otherwise she is my fiancée,' I clarified for her as she looked for the ring on my finger.

She looked aside and thought for a while, then turned back to me, smiling with affection, and said, 'Thank you.'

'Sorry?' I wondered what she meant.

'You know, her face, her brain and her entire body have suffered so much damage . . .'

'Yes, I know.'

'We are trying our best, but there is no guarantee that, for the rest of her life, she will be as beautiful as she was before. You know that too?'

'Yes, I know.'

'That you are standing by her, knowing all this, is what made me thank you . . . In my profession, I have seen several instances where the girls' in-laws tend to break things up with them at the earliest. Being a woman, I understand how much that girl and her family need your support. And more than that I understand how much you love her.'

I was silent for a while. Then, in a shaking voice, I asked her, 'Can you save my love?'

'God will help us all to save your love.' She put her hand on my shoulder, trying to comfort me and raise my hopes.

Then I asked her what I had come to ask her. I explained the condition back home and asked if I should go back to get my mom. 'I am not sure what I should do. I don't want to leave Khushi here in this condition to get my mom.'

'Listen. She is going to need you the most when she opens her eyes. And, with God's grace, if everything goes fine, it will still take four or five days.'

'Four or five days?'

'Yes. Till then, she will be on sedatives. So it's better that you go back and do whatever needs to be done, so that you can come back at the right time. I can understand your mom's state too and I would advice you to go back home, meet your mother and then bring her here.'

Hearing her answer, I made up my mind to go back to my parents and then return to Faridabad by the next week.

The next morning, I saw Khushi for the last time before boarding my plane back to Bhubaneswar. She was calm and unconscious. I kept staring at her face for a while. In my heart, I talked to her. 'I will come back and you will see me when you open your eyes. See you soon, my dear!'

I kissed her hand and I left that place.

Back in my hometown, my presence helped mom get better. Dad too kept encouraging me. We all were going through the worst phase of our lives. Yet, our being together allowed us to stay positive. I saw them praying, every hour of their life, pleading to God to save Khushi's life for me, and for them.

Every few hours I would phone Faridabad. Every time I called up, I was desperate to hear something positive. And three days later, we finally did hear something positive. The doctors revealed that she has shown a considerable amount of improvement. Her blood pressure had stabilized, the platelet count was normal and she was better than she had ever been in the past two weeks, though she still had not regained consciousness.

It was Friday night, I remember.

I thanked God like anything. We all thanked Him. That news brought some happiness to sorrowful faces. After their ambiguous statements, the doctors had started making better remarks now. Even though they still used to end with, 'We believe she is doing good. But to be sure we have to wait till she regains consciousness.'

Therefore, each one of us was waiting for her to open her eyes.

As soon as I got the good news, I boarded the bus to Bhubaneswar. I wanted to book air tickets to Faridabad for my entire family. In haste, I skipped my dinner too. Moments later, I was in the third row, occupying the extreme right seat in the bus. Inside, the lights were turned off. The window pane on my right was open and I could see the moon and the stars shining in the sky. I was happy. I kept staring at the sky for hours before I felt tired enough to sleep. I could feel my eyes getting heavier. I leaned my head against the window and rested for a while.

And then, after several minutes, something strange happened. Something which I could not believe. Shuffling in my sleep, I turned to my left. And I was speechless the next second.

She was sitting right beside me.

Khushi was sitting right beside me.

My shocked eyes kept staring at her. I tried to speak but could not. Hundreds of questions ran through my mind in that one instant and I could not decide which one I should ask first. I looked here and there. In the darkness, every other passenger was sleeping.

She smiled. The accident had left no marks on her face or her body. She appeared so beautiful. Just like she had always been. She was wearing her engagement *sari*.

I was still struggling to understand how this could be.

Very innocently, she put her hand to my forehead, sliding it down to my cheek and resting it there. Then she asked me, 'How are you dear?'

I tried to speak, but my mouth was dry. I swallowed. 'I don't believe this. You were . . . How . . . ?' Those questions remained incomplete.

'I know what you are wondering. But I am here for you. Only for you.'

'But you were far away from me, in Apollo . . . unconscious . . .' I was trying to accept whatever I was seeing.

Gently, she kept answering my queries, 'Shona! I can never be away from you. I was always here, and will always be here. Right beside you, forever.'

I could see her love for me in those eyes. Something in me started believing that whatever was happening was true. I was feeling comfortable and delighted.

After a few moments of silence I spoke, 'I missed you so much, Khushi. For two weeks I couldn't talk to you and you were . . .'

'Shhhhh!' She held her finger to my lips, not allowing me to speak further. 'I know how you've been missing me. I am sorry, dear. That's why, despite all obstacles, I have come to you—the one I love.'

She kissed me.

And then, she had a small box in her hands. I watched her opening it in front of me. It was the engagement ring that she got for me. With her beautiful smile, she brought the ring out and looking up, she took my hand.

'But we will be doing this in front of everyone *na*?' I asked her.

'Nah. I can't wait that long.'

'But why?'

'I don't have much time.'

'What do you mean you don't have much time?'

'Shhh . . . You ask too many questions,' she said, sweetly tweaking my nose. And then, looking straight into my eyes, she continued, 'Because I am dying to be yours . . . Hey, handsome! Will you marry me?'

In that moment of happiness, I could not utter anything. I just nodded.

She slid that beautiful ring onto my third finger and, to my surprise, I noticed the ring I got for her was already on her third finger.

I hugged her and kissed her forehead and lips. We held hands.

After few minutes of romantic silence, she suddenly recalled something. 'Why did you skip your dinner? You are hungry *na*.'

'No, I am not,' I said, but she didn't believe me and opened her bag to get another box out. It was the tiffin-box she used to take to her office.

'See what I have made for you.'

'Hey! *Rajma chawal*!' I almost shouted, troubling the sleeping passengers.

With her own hands she fed me my favorite dish. We kept talking. She, more than I. We shared the last bite after which she said to me,

'Don't skip your meals. You have to take care of yourself.'

I didn't reply. I was feeling her fingers in my hand.

'Promise me,' she said.

'What?' I asked, distracted, making irregular figures on her palm with my fingers, playing with her ring.

'Promise me you will take care of yourself . . . Always.'

'Why?'

Mysteriously, she replied, 'Because I may not be able to bring *rajma chawal* for you all the time.' And she laughed. She looked cute. She kissed me again on my forehead and looked deep into my eyes. I felt something different in that kiss, in her eyes.

And then, just like a kid, she asked me, 'Listen, I want to rest my head on your shoulder for a while.'

And so she rested on my left shoulder. We were still holding hands. A few moments of silence passed. I checked to see if she was asleep while trying to release my hand from hers. She wasn't. She didn't allow me to take my hand away. She wanted me to hold her tight.

I took her in my arms when she said, 'Shona! Thank you for giving me the love of my life.'

I didn't reply, but kissed her hair. We didn't talk much. I wanted her to rest. After so long, we had these moments together. Some more time passed. I don't know how much. And then, all of a sudden, I felt something hitting my forehead.

What was that? I could not understand. But I could hear something. Some sound, some kind of vibration, bothering me. For a few seconds I could not figure out what it was. I was struggling to open my eyes.

I found the window pane on my right was still open and my head was resting against the grill. Maybe I hit my head against it in my sleep. I was regaining my senses. In my pocket, my cellphone was ringing.

It was still dark inside the bus. A gust of wind brought me completely out of my sleep. Outside the sky was calm, the moon was losing its sheen, the stars were disappearing. It was early dawn.

And all of a sudden I realized—the ring was missing from my finger. I immediately turned to my left looking for her. But she wasn't there. I got scared. I stood up and looked here and there in order to find her. But I could not see her. She was gone, I don't know where.

The phone in my pocket was still ringing and in my confusion I quickly pulled it out.

'Khushi calling . . .' it displayed.

I checked my wristwatch. It was 4 a.m. It was an odd time to call.

'It must be urgent,' I thought and picked up the phone. 'Hello?'

But I didn't get any response from the other side, though I could hear somebody's breath.

'Dad?'

'Beta . . .'

I was right. It was Khushi's dad. 'Yes, Dad?' I said.

He spoke after a long silence. 'Beta . . . it's a sad news. Our Khushi is no more. She left us a few minutes back . . .'

'But she was here with me a few minutes back . . .' I heard someone inside me screaming but not a sound came out.

Something heavy stuck my heart, a terrible blow. My eyes widened. I froze. Some kind of coldness crawled within me. My muscles could not move. My heart seemed to alternately stop beating and pump furiously. My brain went numb. I lost control over myself and the echo of that message beat against my eardrums. I don't remember, I can't recall anything else.

'*Waheguru* . . . *Waheguru* . . . *Waheguru* . . .' was all that came out of me, after which the phone fell out of my hands.

I was blank. All that came to my mind was—I need to go back home, to my parents. At the mid-way stop, I got off the bus and boarded one that went back to Burla. A different sort of calm had come over me. I wasn't crying.

When, hours later, I opened the door to my house, I saw my parents staring at me wondering why I was back. I stood there staring back at them in response.

I was still calm.

Then, summoning all my courage, I told them the saddest news of my life.

As soon as mom heard, she gripped my wrist and looked at the pictures of prophets and Gods on our wall in anger. Dad buried his face in his hands. Mom cried, Dad cried and their cries echoed in that room. I was still calm. Or maybe it was a numbness. Nothing seemed to register in my mind. I looked at them for a while and then left them to go into my room.

I lay on my bed, pulling the blanket completely over me. I curled up there, squeezing my hands between my thighs.

I cried.

Without Her

'For past few hours, we were seeing the signs of improvement in her, but all of a sudden her blood pressure fell down drastically. The impact was so much that it led to her heart collapse,' said the doctors.

The family wanted to see her.

The doctors said they couldn't hand over the body to the family.

(Did you notice? Yes, *body*. That's what they said. She no longer had a name. She was just a *body*. A dead body.)

It was an accident and the police had to be involved, there were legal formalities to be taken care of, after which her body was to be taken for the postmortem. The family pleaded with them to spare her from the autopsy, but the authorities drove her to a place where the rest of her mortal remains were torn apart.

Far away from all that was happening, I was still in a state of shock. The truth was so hard to accept. I don't know what happened later, but I could imagine what was happening at her place . . . I heard those cries of pain around me. I saw her fingers, and I clutched at her ring in my right pocket. I saw her being swathed in white and I grabbed her colourful *sari* close to my heart. Something within me was going numb, realizing that I could not be there during her last moments.

Moments later, I could feel that something innocent was being burnt.

I didn't even get a chance to kiss her dead hand . . .

A dead silence persisted in my house. Unlike me, my parents cried in private, for they had to strengthen me. They didn't even get to see the girl their son wanted to marry.

In the evening, Dad booked the tickets and the next day, both of us left for Faridabad.

A day later, in the afternoon, I opened the door to their house. Amidst everyone (I didn't know them all), I noticed her mom and I rushed to hug her, before we both burst into tears.

The irony of it . . . The home, which was going to sparkle in celebration of their daughter's engagement, had such a different atmosphere now. People in dull clothes sat on a giant mattress on the floor of the vacant drawing room. There were whispers and there were sudden cries. And there were those eyes in which the tears had dried up. A curse had fallen upon us all.

Amid the ordeal of surviving without her, at her home, the very place where she was brought up and nurtured, my day passed somehow. Evening approached. More distant relatives, more acquaintances had arrived. And this led to more cries and more tears. Seeing all this, I wanted to run away to some place where I could be alone with just her memories for company . . . to room 301 maybe . . .

Everything was so unbelievable. Yet, it was real.

It got dark at about eight. I was at a photo-studio getting a picture of my dead girlfriend framed, to keep in the *gurudwara* during the last prayer for her, scheduled for the next day. Guess which picture . . . ?

It was one of those, which she stayed awake till dawn to send me, when I was in my US office. Never in my worst nightmare could I have thought that someday I'd be using her picture for this purpose.

When the shopkeeper handed me the frame, I happened to look into her eyes in that picture. They were beautiful.

Seconds later, I felt Ami di's fingers wiping my wet eyelashes. We paid and left for home.

The next day, we all assembled in the *gurudwara*. A last prayer for the peace of her departed soul. The moment I entered, my gaze fell upon her photograph which was now decked with flowers. No one on earth would want to see his girlfriend's picture decked with flowers. It just kills you. And it's so hard to face this truth again and again and, yet, restrain yourself in front of everybody.

She still appeared so beautiful.

Everyone gathered there was dressed in white. A few people were praying. When I passed by the row of ladies, I heard a few murmurs, 'This is the guy who was going to marry her.'

I heard but I ignored them and made my way to the extreme corner, away from my dad, her dad, her family and God.

I don't remember what happened and for how long I was there. I was with her in my memories. And, subconsciously, I was following the actions of the others. When they stood up, I stood up. When they bowed, I bowed. In a few hours, I think, it was all over . . . except for the pain in my aching heart.

Back at her home that afternoon, the family which was to host a dinner celebrating the engagement was now hosting her funeral lunch. The cooks who had been booked to prepare a lavish cuisine were now preparing something else. The people who got engagement invitations a few days ago were now gathered for such a different reason. And where was I . . . ?

Serving lunch to the people who didn't even know me.

In the corner of that room, I saw my own fate mocking me.

The day ended and the night arrived again. And while I wished that her soul may rest in peace, my own soul was restless within. I was trying to sleep, but sleep was far from me. Images from the time I had spent with her kept running through my mind for a long time. That's the last thing I remember. I don't know when that far away sleep came near and embraced me.

'Hey! He is back!'

'Ooooooohhh! Come on, everybody. Ravin's back after his engagement.'

Two days later, I was back in my office. Apart from one or two people, no one was aware how reality had drastically changed for me, how things were so different from what everyone assumed.

And, unaware, my friends and colleagues rushed to me the moment they saw me coming out of the elevator on our floor. In no time, before I could say anything, I found myself enclosed in an irregular circle of people. They were shouting, singing and demanding a treat from me.

I stood silently.

Someone shouted, 'Hey, show us your ring.' Someone else in the crowd pulled at my right hand, looking for it.

I still stood silently.

But the entire floor kept looking at the gathering around me. From far away, a few folks shouted, 'Congrats! Buddy.'

'Where is the ring? Did you forget it in the shower? Or have you dumped it in some bank's locker?'

'Hahahaha!'

'Hey, come on. Speak up.'

And I was looking at the floor, watching nothing, gathering the strength to speak.

'If she gets to know that you aren't wearing her ring, isn't she gonna shout at you?' someone joked.

And I looked up to face them all. Some of them noticed my damp eyes and they stopped their jokes.

'She will never shout at me,' I said softly to the people in front of me. A few heard, a few did not.

'Why not? Have you started scaring her?' asked a voice from behind me. 'Hahahaha!'

I turned and faced everybody. My eyes told them my misery. And I just managed to say, 'Because she is no more.'

She died. I survived.

Because I survived, I died everyday.

I was bound by my stars to live a lonely life. Without her, I felt so alone. Though the fact is that it's just *she* who is gone and everything else is the same. But this 'everything else' is nothing to me . . .

I miss her in my days. I miss her in my nights. I miss her every moment of my life.

And I'll tell you what this loneliness feels like, what it feels like to live a life without the person you loved more than anything or anyone else in the world:

Recalling something about her, you happen to laugh and in no time, sometimes even as you laugh, you taste your own tears.

The more you want to avoid romance around you, the more you will find it. It will torture you. You will see couples kissing and hugging each other, resting their heads on each other's shoulders. You will see them everywhere, even in the movie halls where you'll want to spend a few hours in darkness. You will find a pair sitting next to you, doing all that you, some time in the past, did with your beloved. You will feel pain, your heart will bleed. And, very calmly, you will walk on pretending you didn't see anything.

Your friends will talk about yet another hot chick. But all the good-looking girls on this planet will fail to attract you. Nothing excites you, even your sexual desires go into hibernation. While working out in the gym, you will try to lift the heaviest weights. Later, standing under the shower, you will cry hard but nobody will hear you. The splashing of the shower will mask the sounds of your sobbing.

You will search for and consume anything that can erase your memory.

And, believe me, your life will appear worse than death.

Every thing that brought a smile to my face had now started torturing me. Even the Shaadi.com ads on the Internet added to my agony. I remember how she used to tell me that, after our marriage, we would put a success story on the website. I never knew I would be writing a tragedy.

At times, I felt like a drug addict who badly needs his next hit. But at least an addict has his drugs . . . I felt suffocated. As if something was stopping my breath. As if something was choking my soul.

I got scared of things. I don't know what they were, but they wouldn't let me sleep. And, like a kid, I'd rush to my mom, to sleep beside her. She would pat my forehead. Still, for hours, I would stare at the fan rotating above me.

If ever I fell asleep, I would wake to nightmares, screaming. The time was always 4 a.m.

The Present

20 July 2007

A very special day. A day of celebration and mourning.

Another evening arrives, so similar and so different from the one exactly a year ago. This evening, I am recalling that evening, when I received her first SMS, when we talked for the first time, on the phone. Wanting to know—from someone, everyone and no one—why I had to live both these evenings. Life would have been bliss, if I were to live only one of them, but not both. Had the second not arrived, I would have been kissing my engagement ring, talking to her, celebrating a year of being together. Had the first not arrived, there would have been no second one.

It was raining then and it is raining today as well. I didn't have a love life then and I have none, now. I never wished to have someone so special or to become so special to someone then, nor do I feel that way today.

But that evening she was talking to me, questioning me, laughing at my sense of humor, but she is not doing that today. I didn't know her at all then, today she lives somewhere close to my soul.

When I look back, I laugh and cry over those moments. They bring back such mixed feelings that make me so restless.

Should I celebrate or should I weep? Look what I had, look what I lost . . .

I remember, while talking to her, how I had brandished my invisible sword in the air in front of an invisible audience, and announced like a king, 'This day will be celebrated throughout the nation and declared a public holiday henceforth. Schools and colleges will remain closed on this day. This will be a second Valentine's Day for people in love.'

And she had laughed at my craziness.

When I look back now, I am relieved that I wasn't a king and there was no real audience for, had they come to me now and asked me to celebrate, I would have no answers.

Here I am, feeling so alone even in the most crowded of places. And without my better half, this remaining half is getting worse day by day. So much pain, so much grief . . . Even the tears have dried up.

But still, I have to sustain myself, I have to live and I have to laugh . . .

And, therefore, on this day in my office when there is nobody on my floor, I open her picture on my computer. I tease her, pinch her nose, run my fingers over her eyes, cheeks and beautiful lips, kiss her passionately again after so long and say, 'Congratulations! We've now been a couple for a year. Three days of fighting and 362 days of love. Not that bad *haan*?'

And I run to the washroom to wash away my tears. I don't want to cry today.

The day passes in an effort to laugh and to be happy by any means. Now night has arrived. Lying down on my bed, I wonder . . . If I were in her place and she in mine, what would her life have been like? Would she have been able to survive without me? Would she be living just for the sake of living, for the sake of her family, the way I do now? Would she still have faith in

God, which I lost long back? Would her family be thinking of another match for her? Would she, one day, forget me?

One year later

Things around me have returned to what they were some two years ago, before Khushi came into my life. The romantic movies on my video shelf have been replaced by action movies. I am sleeping on time, as there are no late-night calls now. My Orkut status has rolled back from 'committed' to 'single'. I didn't want to change it because I still feel committed to her. But the awkward questions from people on my scrapbook made me.

With her, everything else has gone—my dreams, my happiness, my good-looking future and a lot more. I have changed (of course, people tend to). It's been almost a year since I've laughed. But I have learnt to wear a fake smile. It's very difficult, but it makes my parents feel that I am getting better, even though I know I'm not. I don't talk much. When I am with friends, I want to be alone. When I am alone, I want company. Nothing comforts.

With the arrival of night and the passing of each day, I realize that another day of my lonely life has gone. So, I am now little closer to the world where she has gone.

And people, especially my relatives, have started to say that I should get married, that my condition is not good. They don't have the courage to say that to my face, so they hint at it, subtly. My parents (just like anybody else's) want to see me happy. They also feel that only some other girl could console me and make me forget everything and start a new life.

But, another girl?

What would I tell her? That I spent the best hour of my life in the lap of a girl who is not you? That I may have married you but I'm still in love with a girl who doesn't exist? That whatever you do, every time I compare you with her, even when you kiss me? Won't I be screwing up so many lives—the girl's, her family's, my family's. And mine? But mine is already screwed up.

I keep asking myself these questions. And because I don't have any answers to them, I walk away whenever this subject comes up. And then my mom and dad ask me, 'Where are you going?'

'I don't know,' I say.

'How long are you going to escape these questions *beta*? You've got to settle down some day.'

'I don't feel like it,' I say. Then, after a long pause, 'All right, I am getting late. I am leaving to see a friend of mine.'

'Wait! You have to answer us. Why can't you think again of settling down? Why can't you think of a different girl?'

'I cannot, Dad.'

'But why not?'

'Because . . .' and I stop and walk away from the discussion and my home.

In the background, I hear my Dad shouting the same question 'But why not?'

'Because, to think of another girl, I feel like a whore,' I silently say to the emptiness around me.

~

I am in my neighborhood park. It is early morning. After a long jog I am resting on a bench. There is a woman sitting next to me. I don't know her.

She is knitting a red sweater. She is with her daughter who is on the see-saw with another boy in that park. She is probably six years old.

There are a lot of people in the park. A lot of kids too. I don't know any of them.

I am lost in thought, with my hands underneath my chin. The see-saw, right in front of my eyes, has become blurred. My eyes don't move. Interrupting my thoughts, I hear the loud voice of the woman sitting next to me.

'Don't do that! Sit properly or you'll fall.'

In front of my unfocussed eyes, the blurred see-saw is rising up and going down. Then it speeds up and I hear the same voice again.

'Don't do that, you will fall . . . No . . . No . . . Noooo!'

All of sudden, the other side of the see-saw doesn't come up. It stops abruptly.

The little girl is lying on the ground. I am trying to understand what has happened.

Her mother sitting next to me cries her name.

Her name . . .

I know that name.

And, suddenly, I am scared. I look at her and then at her daughter. I run to help her. I am worried and breathing heavily. I kneel to lift her up. She is not crying. I check her face, her hands and legs for cuts and scrapes. Innocently, she says she is fine. I am cleaning the dirt from her clothes. There is a tear in my eye. I hold her face in my hands and tell her that it is good she is fine and I smile.

Her worried mother reaches us and takes her in her arms. I stand up and see she has dropped that half-knit sweater on the ground. She is kissing her forehead. I go back and pick the sweater up for her.

I want to make sure if what I heard was correct or just my imagination. I ask her, 'What's your name?'

Helping her hair behind her ear, exactly in the same way, she says in her cute voice, 'My name is Khushi.'

I keep staring at her for a while. Her mother looks at me.

I tell her, 'It's a beautiful name.'

Then I walk back home.

~

Acknowledgements

My sincere thanks to the following people, for taking me ahead in the journey of writing this book.

Khushi's Dad, for reviewing this book for the very first time and helping me with his first edit work.

Priyanka Rathee, my colleague, my good friend, for being punctual at the 4 o'clock evening tea at *Udupi* in our campus, where she used to pen down those beautiful prose pieces for this book.

Ridhima Arora, my cutest and dearest friend, for being the kind of a reader who can be any writer's delight. For always keeping my spirits up and showing me the better ways to bring this book up.

Glossary of Punjabi Terms

Page	Hindu word/phrase	English translation
ix	Tere jaane ka asar kuch aisa hua mujh par, tujhe dhoondate dhoondate, maine khud ko paa liya	Such was the devastation of your going away, that in the desperation of looking for you, I found myself
3	veeeeeeer	my brotherrrr
19	Bismil ka sandesh hai ki kal Lahore jaane wali gaadi hum Kakori pe lootenge, aur un paison se hathiyar kharidenge	Bismil has messaged that we will loot tomorrow's train to Lahore in Kakori and then buy weapons from that money
29	haan?	right?
30	Bye *nahin*, see you	Don't say 'bye', say 'see you'
32	Shona	Sweetheart
35	chapatti	Indian bread
	Hai na?	Right?
36	baba	honey/sweetheart (in this case)

37	na?	right?
38	Chalo	Okay
	Shonimoni	Sweetheart
41	tumhe ungli kya pakdai, tum to pura haath pakdna chahte ho. Zyaada galat fehmiyaan mat paalo	give someone an inch and they'll take a mile. Don't you dare imagine anything more
42	Haath pakdna?	Hold your hand?
	haan?	right?
	Mera baby uth gaya?	My baby has woken up?
43	Aaye-haye . . . haye . . .	Oh my god
	Achcha baba	Okay, honey
44	Sachhi?	Really?
	Muchhi	Really
	Jaaaaan	My looove
	chamatkaar	some magical reason
45	Haan	Yes
	Shona, ek minute	Sweetheart, one minute
	ek minute	one minute
	chamatkaar	magical reason
	meri jaan	my love
46	baba	honey
47	Bolo karoge na?	Say you will do it?
55	Haanji	Yes
	theek hai	all right

56	Yeh lo, ladki vaalon ki taraf se	Take this, it's from the bride's side
58	na?	right?
59	Safar mein koi takleef to nahi hui?	Hope you had no problem during your journey?
	Suniye ji, aapke safar mein ...	Listen, during your journey ...
	nahi koi takleef nahi hui	no, I didn't have any problems
63	Haan bolo?	Yes, what are you saying?
	yaar	term used for addressing a friend/also addressing someone casually (colloquial)
	Arey, I know baba	I know, sweetie
65	pehla nasha, pehla khumaar; naya pyaar hai, naya imtihaan	first drink and then it's stupor; it's a new love with new challenges (lyrics from a film song)
66	na	right
67	gurudwara	Sikh place of worship
68	Aisa hi hota	This is what happens
69	Aisa hi hota	This is what happens
	Kuch nahin	Nothing
	Lo aa gaya aapka sasuraal	Here, we've reached your in-laws' house
	kada	holy bracelet

69	Sat Sri Akal	Trust in the ultimate God (it's a type of greeting in Punjabi)
	Sat Sri Akal beta ji	Greetings to you, my son
	Baitho beta	Sit, son
	Main bas abhi aayi	I'll be right back
70	sasuraal	in-law's house
	baaraat	wedding procession
	doli	palanquin
	shehnai	a musical instrument
	Saali	Sister in law
71	Sirf aapke liye hi	Just for you
	samosa	a fried snack with potato filling
	Haanji beta, lo na	Yes, please take one, son
	aloo bhujiya	potato fritters
	dhokla	gujrati snack
	Arey, aap to kuch le hi nahi rahe ho . . . Yeh lo na	You are not taking anything . . . take this please
	Nahin	No
	bas, bas, bas	that's enough
	Lo, ho gai taiyaar maharaani	Behold, the queen is dressed now
	kameez	long shirt worn by women
	pyjaami	pyjama made for women
	chunni	stole

72	chunni	stole
	dhokla	gujrati snack
	rasgullas	cottage cheese balls dipped in sugar syrup (served as sweet)
	aa gayi	elder sister has come
73	Unke saath hi to aayi hongi	She would have come with him/them
74	Pata hai, Jiju bahut achcha khaana banaate hain	You should know your brother in law makes great food
	Beta aap khaana bana lete ho?	Son, can you cook?
75	salwar kameez	Indian long shirt and loose pants for women
	Arey, kuch gaa ke sunao na?	Why don't you sing something for us?
	paranthas	Indian stuffed bread
	Kaun kaun se paranthe?	Which all stuffed bread can you make?
76	aloo ke, pyaaz ke	potato ones, onion ones
	gobhi ke	cauliflower ones
	mooli ke bhi	radish ones too
	rajma	kidney beans curry
	paneer, raita, aloo gobhi	cottage cheese, flavoured curds, potato and cauliflower
77	chapattis	Indian bread
	rajma	kidney beans curry

77	Chapatti	Indian bread
	Chapatti	Indian bread
	Chapatti	Indian bread
	rajma	kidney beans curry
79	yaar	term used for addressing a friend/also addressing someone casually (colloquial)
80	na?	right?
	Class to hai	I do have a class
81	na?	right?
	Chalo	Come
83	na	right
	Mataji to dairy tak jaayengi. Aur aap kahan tak jaaoge? Delhi tak?	Mother will go to the milk dairy/shop. Till where will you go? Up to Delhi?
	Nahin bhaiyya, yeh to IMS pe hi utar jaayegi	No, brother, she will get off at IMS
	Ye to IMS pe hi utar jayegi matlab? Tuney kahaan utarna hai fir?	What do you mean she will get off at IMS? Then where will you get off?
84	Gayi bhains paani mein	Oh hell
	Theek hai?	Okay?
	Marte marte bache hain. Ye bhi naa	We nearly died. You are a fool
91	na	right
	Bhaiyya	Brother

92	Bhaiyya	Brother
	Kuch keh nahin sakte, madam. Bahut baarish hui hai. Bus aagey road pe kahin jam na laga ho.	Can't say anything, madam. It's rained a lot. Hopefully, we shouldn't get a jam ahead.
	Madam, ghabraane waali to koi baat hi nahin hai. Hum pahanch jaayenge.	Madam, no need to worry. We will reach.
93	yaar	term used for addressing a friend/also addressing someone casually (colloquial)
	na?	right?
	haan baba	yes, sweetie
	Theek hai	Okay
94	Theek hai?	All right?
	Sahib ab nikal jaayenge aaraam se, jam khul gaya hai. Bas ek baar border cross kar lein. Phir highway theek hai.	Sir, now we will be able to move comfortably, the jam has eased off. Just need to cross the border. Then highway should be smooth.
95	Bataao na, Shona	tell me please, sweetie
	Shona	Sweetie
	na . . . kya baat hai	right . . . what is the matter
98	Bhaiyya	Brother
	Sahib ye choti gaadi hai, engine mein paani chala jaayega. Hum aur aagey nahin jaa sakte.	Sir, this is a small car, the water enters the engine very quickly, we can't go any further.

98	Bhaiyya. Is vakt na, mera dimaag bahot jaada kharaab ho raha hai, aur agar fir se tumne ye kaha naa ...	Brother, I am very upset at this moment and if you say this once more ...
99	Bhaiyya, mujhe sirf inhe ghar tak pahonchaana hai. Aap please aagey chalte raho. Agar aapki cab kharaab hui to jo bhi kharcha hoga vo main de dunga.	Brother, I just want to drop her home. You please keep moving. If your cab breaks down, I'll pay for everything.
	Yeh to hona hi tha	This had to happen
100	Tere baap ki sadak hai? Abey saaley peeche hatt! Arey teri maa ki ...	Do you own this damn road? Bloody idiot, move back. Motherfuckers ...
	Mumma, main IMS mein nahin hun. Main Ravin ke saath hun ... shaam se. I am sorry ki maine aapko jhoot bola.	Mom, I'm not at IMS. I'm with Ravin since evening. I'm sorry I lied.
101	Munnabhai	(It's a movie title)
	Shona ... Sambhal ke ... Dhyaan se	Sweetie ... Careful ... More carefully
	Sahib aur jor se	Sir, put more effort and push
102	Sahib aur jor se	Sir, with more effort
103	Bhaiyya yahaan par jaraa dhyaan se	Brother, a bit carefully here

105	walla	puller
	Chal	Come
	Khushi ki koi galti nahi hai is mein. Ye saara plan mera tha.	Khushi is not at fault here. This was my plan entirely.
106	Ise itna pyaar karti hu naa, isliye itni chinta hoti hai iski. Thodey dino mein chale jaana hai isne yahaa se aapke ghar . . .	I love her too much, that is why I worry about her so much. In a few days she will leave this home, and go to yours . . .
	Munnabhai	(It's a movie title)
108	Uth gaya mela baby?	Has my baby woken up?
109	Wudgyaa	(Would you is being said in an American accent here)
115	desi	Indian
	Munnabhai	(It's a movie title)
	gyaan	sage advice
117	Kab aaoge Shona	When will you come, sweetie
118	Achchi lag rahi hu na main?	I'm looking good, right?
	Bahut!	Amazing!
120	Mujhe bhi do . . . maine bhi baat karni hai	Give it to me . . . I want to talk too
122	RUKO!	STOP!
125	Cold hua hai tumhe?	Are you down with cold?
	Nah	Nope

127	Sachhi?	Really?
	Mucchi	Really
129	Chalo!	Come!
	Haanji	Yes, sir
	Aap Khushi maasi ke dost ho . . . hain . . . aap ho na?	You are Khushi's aunt's friend, right?
	Aao na . . . Maasi aapke liye tayaar ho rahi hai . . . Aao . . . Aao	Come . . . Aunty's getting dressed for you . . . Come . . . Come
131	Mujhe bhi jaana hai . . . Mujhe bhi jaana hai!	I want to go too . . . I want to go too!
	Tu bhi saath mein chali jaa	You should go along with them
132	diyas	earthen lamps
136	jamun	black berries
137	jamun	black berries
	Batao naa	Tell me
	Kamaal hai	Too much
	aur haan	and one more thing
138	Jawahar Minaar	(This is the name of a tower.)
141	Arey	Hey
142	Arey buddhu!	Hey, silly!
	yaar	term used for addressing a friend/also addressing someone casually (colloquial)

142	Achcha	Okay
	Arey, dekthe reh jaaoge	Hey, you will be amazed
	Arey	Hey
143	kahin kuch	something somewhere
146	yaar	term used to address a friend
147	na?	right?
151	sari	Indian dress
152	bhangra	A dance style from Punjab in India
154	Sat Sri Akal	Trust in the ultimate God (a type of greeting from Punjab)
158	beta ji	son
159	maasis	aunts
161	Saas–Bahu	Television serials involving stories between mother-in-laws and daughter-in-laws
171	Sat Sri Akal, beta	Trust in the ultimate God, son (a type of greeting from Punjab)
172	veer	brother
	yaar	term used for addressing a friend/also addressing someone casually (colloquial)
	bhangra	A dance style from Punjab in India

175	Mahavir Jayanti	Birth Anniversay of Lord Mahavir
183	sari	Indian dress
184	na?	right?
185	na	right
	Rajma chawal	Kidney beans curry and rice
187	Waheguru	Wonderful lord
188	sari	Indian dress
189	gurudwara	Sikh place of worship
190	gurudwara	Sikh place of worship
195	haan?	right?
197	beta	child